A BAKER STREET MYSTERY

THE CASE OF

THE INVISIBLE THIEF

Thomas Brace Haughey

Bethany Fellowship INC.
MINNEAPOLIS, MINNESOTA 55438

The Case of the Invisible Thief
by Thomas Brace Haughey
Illustrations by Ken Lochhead

Library of Congress Catalog Card Number 78-68424

ISBN 0-87123-086-0

DIMENSION BOOKS
Published by Bethany Fellowship, Inc.
6820 Auto Club Road, Minneapolis, Minnesota 55438

Printed in the United States of America

DEDICATION

To John Warwick Montgomery, the first Geoffrey Weston fan. Without his encouragement Sleuths Ltd. might never have opened its doors for business.

ABOUT THE AUTHOR

THOMAS BRACE HAUGHEY is the English Program Director of missionary radio station KVMV-FM in McAllen, Texas. He received his Bachelor's degree from the University of Maryland, in 1965, and a Th.M. from Capital Bible Seminary in 1969. In addition he received a diploma from Rio Grande Bible Institute Language School. While at the University of Maryland he was inducted into the literary honorary society, Phi Delta Epsilon. He has done evangelism and youth work in Mexico, and taught for a year and one half in a missionary Bible School. His experience as a writer includes: Editing a Jesus Paper, writing numerous articles, writing scripts for FOLK FESTIVAL, a weekly radio program, and more than 100 book reviews each year for broadcast. Mr. Haughey is married, the father of one daughter, and makes his home in McAllen, Texas.

PREFACE

Ever since Edgar Allan Poe popularized "who-done-its," Americans have loved them. And so has the rest of the world. There's nothing quite like sitting in an easy chair and matching wits with a master detective! Danger mounts. Suspense builds. Did the butler do it, or could Aunt Agatha have fired the shot?

Even in war time, detective mania has persisted. Both Abraham Lincoln and F.D.R. read mysteries during their troubled administrations. As daily reports of battlefield carnage poured in, the two no doubt sought relief from the strain of command. They sometimes found it in that ordered world where clue follows clue until violence is subdued. Meanwhile, soldiers in the trenches relaxed in front of—you guessed it—detective novels. Escapism? Entertainment? Of course! But that's only part of the story. In war or in peace there's just something satisfying about seeing a villain get his comeuppance.

Medieval morality plays conveyed a simple truth. Virtue pays. Sin destroys. That same theme lies at the heart of virtually every detective story worthy of the name. Crime is followed by doing time. The good get the goods on the hoods. And readers love it. Deep down inside they know that situational ethics is baloney. And they welcome the simplicity of clear-cut right and wrong.

Not all detectives, of course, have been pillars of virtue. The Saint was less than saintly. Holmes smoked dope. And Bond was a Casanova. But each fought against an evil even greater than his own. Other detectives have been decidedly nice people. Perry Mason is one of my favorites. Then there's the sprightly old Miss Marple. A few part-timers have even been members of the clergy. The essential ingredients for being a detective, it seems, are a keen mind and a sense of justice.

Sleuths come in every color, shape, and tax bracket. They are fat, thin, old, young, athletic, paralyzed, black, white, yellow, rich and poverty stricken. But even in the midst of that motley crew, Geoffrey Weston stands out. He has a twinkle in his eye and a talent for puns. He also prays. To my knowledge he's the only detective old enough to vote who—as Jimmy Carter would put it—has been born again. Weston battles evil with a passion. In this—his latest adventure—a skirmish or two almost cost him his life. But enough said. Pit your own deductive powers against his as you try to solve *The Case of the Invisible Thief.*

TABLE OF CONTENTS

CHAPTER 1

Stolen Through Steel

That morning the kitchen was fairly presentable. There had not been a mystery of note for several weeks, and we had been driven by inactivity to taking up the broom, mop, and dishrag. Geoffrey Weston sat across from me at the breakfast table—munching a jelly-laden muffin. His interest, though, centered on the early edition of the *Times* spread before him.

"John, what do you make of this?" With a frown he thrust the paper toward me. His boney forefinger pointed to a short piece on page five.

Sabotage at Dorking

Research papers turned up missing last night at the Pinehurst Laboratory near Dorking. Dr. Arthur Heath, director of the facility, has assured local authorities, however, that the materials were neither of military nor of commercial value. No motive has as yet been determined for the alleged theft. Scotland Yard, however, is far more puzzled as to the "how" than as to the "why" of the affair. The papers, it seems, disappeared from a safe in a sealed room under twenty-four-hour surveillance by the Metropol Security Agency. Representatives of Metropol refuse comment on the matter.

I reread the article a time or two and wiped orange jelly off page four before folding the *Times* and setting it aside.

"Weston, there's more to this than meets the eye. Scotland Yard wouldn't be bothering with the case if it were merely a curiosity. And why is a theft classed as sabotage?"

Geoffrey propped up his chin with his right arm and stared at the web a spider was industriously spinning in one corner of the ceiling.

"Excellent, John. Why, indeed? I found that heading most peculiar. The *Times* has a long tradition to uphold. They are not noted for inferior journalism. Yet titles are meant to summarize stories—and this title does not do that. Sabotage at Dorking! It's almost as though the heading were meant for some other story."

"Perhaps," I suggested, "since they've started having computers set the type, the title actually is for another—"

"No," Weston interrupted, "that won't do. None of the account rings true." He compressed his lips and slowly shook his head. "Unimportant papers are not locked in a safe and guarded by Metropol. Thieves do not perpetrate an impossible crime for nothing. Laboratory directors do not tell local police that a theft is unimportant and then go and call the Yard—that is, unless they're hiding something."

"But maybe it was the locals who asked for help," I prompted.

Geoffrey smiled. "And why would they do that, John? Why bother outsiders if the stolen papers were worthless? Do you know what I think? I think those papers were deucedly important—so important that we are reading managed news. I think some reporter followed the police dispatcher's directions to Pinehurst

Laboratory, got a story, called it in, and later had it quashed by someone with influence."

"Then why was it printed at all?"

"A good question!" Geoffrey conceded. "I'm not sure of the answer. But I have a feeling the maneuvering was done just before the *Times* went to bed—at around three this morning. Tired people were making snap decisions. Perhaps the editor refused to back down completely. One thing is certain. The rewrite was a rush job. The copy editor retained the old title."

"Then you think—"

"I think that the word 'sabotage' fits. I don't think Pinehurst Laboratory can function normally without the information in those documents. And if I were a betting chap, I would wager that we are going to hear more about this matter."

"You expect that we'll be consulted?"

"Let me put it this way," Geoffrey replied smiling. "We are about to throw the mop in a corner, forget about the broom, and let that little fellow over there spin on in peace. There's a web of intrigue in Dorking, and we're going to catch someone in it."

With almost a flourish, he dug his fork into a plate of scrambled eggs. We ate on in silence. After a few moments we heaped our dishes into an artistic pile in the sink and escaped to the living room. While Geoffrey busied himself with the remainder of the paper, I put a record on the console and relaxed. My thoughts wandered back some six months to the rental of our present quarters and the first posting of our advertisement in the London dailies:

Sleuths, Ltd.
London's Consulting Detective Firm
Number 31, Baker Street

I had suggested waiting for installation of the telephone before publicizing. But Geoffrey opposed the idea. He detested receiving frivolous calls. And I think he rather enjoyed the distinction that an unlisted number drew between himself and London's assemblage of detectives for hire. He took delight in recreating the rustic air that so characterized his grandfather Mycroft's celebrated brother. Our selection of a Baker Street office completed the picture. It lent us a mystique that had attracted clients. God had been good to us. Business had been adequate. And we were, you might say, "comfortably fixed." But at this point my woolgathering was interrupted by Geoffrey's voice.

"We may be well off, John, but if I worked for money I fear I would go mad in a week. How many poor souls work only for a salary and live and die as slaves—without even knowing what they are? It's the calling that counts for everything—knowing you're doing what you're designed for and what you enjoy doing. Hang the money! Matching wit against wit and putting puzzles together—that's the life for me!" He leaned back and sighed—savoring the thought.

"Weston," I exclaimed, "you've done it again! A man around here can't have a thought to himself! What did I do this time—glance at the ledger?"

"Indeed you did, old fellow. And there was no mistaking that sigh of satisfaction or your patting your well-filled stomach. And there was that prolonged gaze in the direction of the telephone table. I can only conclude that you feel we've done fairly well even with an unlisted number. But ho! Who's that walking by our window? Well, well, if it isn't Inspector Twigg! And he's not alone. John, be so good as to pour extra cups of tea. We have company."

As I retreated to the kitchen cupboard, Geoffrey

made his way to the door, skirting some of those obstacles which tend to collect in bachelor quarters. In a moment he returned, ushering in our guests. I greeted our visitors with a wave of the hand as I busied myself in the kitchen. Geoffrey made the introductions.

"Dreadfully sorry about leaving the gate locked, Twigg! It's been years since the Irish Republicans went in for violence, but I still take precautions. Old habits rarely die. You remember, of course, my colleague John Taylor, Esq. For the benefit of your friend, let me say I'm Geoffrey Weston. And I take it, Inspector, that this is Dr. Arthur Heath." The Scotland Yard detective's lips compressed into one of his pained "here's another theatrical stunt" expressions.

"Ah, then you've seen the article in the papers, Weston. But how did you guess I'd bring the doctor around?"

"There's very little guesswork about it, actually. When I read in the paper that a laboratory has been burgled (and that the police are without clues) and then—not ten minutes later—find a minion of the law on my doorstep hauling in tow a middle-aged gentleman with a slide rule protruding from his suit-coat pocket, I should be dull indeed not to reach the obvious conclusion."

"Quite so, Weston—unless the doctor had sent an assistant. Let me say bluntly that we have come to seek your help. Mr. Heath has agreed to pay your usual consultation fee. But I believe you'd even take up this matter if it were you who had to pay. There's been nothing like it in England since the disappearance of Jessica Worthington's corpse."

"You intrigue me, Twigg. Pray, be seated, gentlemen. And Mr. Heath, be good enough to fill in the details and correct the misstatements of the newspaper article. Start from the beginning. Try to leave nothing out—no matter how inconsequential it may seem. John has some tea brewing, so please take your time. Would you care, sir, for sugar or honey, one teaspoon or two?"

"Two of honey, please."

I brought the cups to the overstuffed chairs in which Weston had seated our visitors. It was his custom to, as much as possible, relax the clients. We have learned from experience that a little relaxation can add vital details to any story. Returning with Geoffrey's cup and mine, I cleared a couple of books off a living room chair and sat with the group.

We must have made an interesting tableau. The room was a study in contrasts from its Victorian chairs and early American wall clock to the Danish modern console and our laboratory equipment. The four of us reflected that same diversity. Geoffrey, with his auburn goatee, tall, lanky frame and gaunt features, had the air of an artist or, perhaps, of a college professor. Only the hawkish intensity of his gaze betrayed his true profession. I, on the other hand, am rather a marshmallow of a man—short, a bit portly, and with a ready smile. Twigg radiated chunky strength and determination. He reminded me of a bulldog. Arthur Heath was quite the opposite. His small, slender physique seemed perpetually agitated by inner conflicts. His hands seldom stopped moving. If I likened him to any animal, it would be to a sparrow. Our client, after looking searchingly at each of us, began his account.

"There's not very much to say, really. I left work at the usual hour—at, oh, about six in the afternoon. The papers were in the safe at that time. I saw them when I locked up. After supper I tried some reading and then watched television. I couldn't concentrate. You know how it is with research. One tries doing something one way, and the experiment fails. So he keeps thinking of alternate methods and imagines what their outcome might be. I tried to sleep but found myself staring at the ceiling. So I decided to return to the laboratory and try out some new ideas.

"The guards let me in at a little after half-past one in the morning. I was about to fill a test tube when I noticed a piece of paper lying on the floor in front of the wall safe. I was, quite naturally, curious. We use the safe almost exclusively to house sensitive documents. When I bent down, I discovered a paper that had been locked away for weeks! The safe proved absolutely empty— picked clean. I rang immediately for the police and then confronted the guards. They had either been grossly negligent or were a party to the crime!"

"And why, doctor," Geoffrey queried, "did you believe the guards responsible?"

"Mr. Weston, they simply had to have had a hand in it. The room cannot, I repeat, CANNOT be entered without the guards knowing about it. Both the room and the corridor outside are covered by closed circuit television. The wires from the cameras are encased in a concrete wall and lead directly to the guards' office. The guards work in teams—with both watching the screens. And the corridor is further protected by an invisible light beam cutting across it. An alarm sounds in the guards' office when the beam is broken."

"What of windows?"

"There are none."

"And the material of the walls?"

"Every wall in the building is of reinforced concrete. Even if someone had broken through with an air hammer, he would have been seen."

"And," Geoffrey concluded, "obviously the interior walls of the safe were undamaged since, as you say, the telltale paper was lying on the floor IN FRONT of the safe."

"Absolutely."

"What of the cameras themselves?"

"They are Philips LDK 11's—somewhat old but completely reliable."

"That's a color camera, I believe."

"Yes, it is. And a good one. When I entered the guards' office, the pictures were clear and sharp."

"Do you," Weston asked, "have videotape machines hooked into the circuit?"

"Yes, we do, but they have obviously been altered. They show only myself."

"And are you in the habit of making night visits?"

"No. Only rarely."

At this point Twigg broke into the conversation.

"Weston, we've examined that videotape until we're blue in the face. But we can find no evidence that it has been spliced or that the machine was stopped and re-started. In fact, since the tape shows a clock on the laboratory wall whose hands do not lose a single second, we must conclude that the tape is accurate. It can't be something substituted from the night before, either. It records Dr. Heath picking up the paper and opening the safe. There was no time to dub that in and syncronize the clock. And how would the guards have gotten the papers out of the laboratory? The building is in a brightly lit clearing surrounded by a ten-foot fence and patrolled by three additional guards. There is no way they could have gotten the stuff out."

Arthur Heath, who had been shaking his head throughout the Inspector's comments, was obviously unconvinced.

"I don't know how they did it," Heath conceded. "Maybe ALL the guards were implicated. Or perhaps

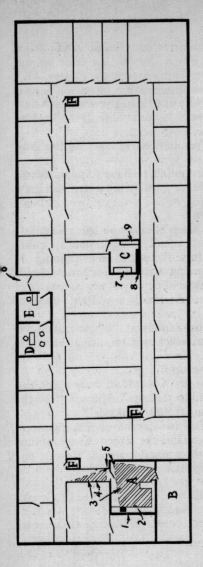

MAIN BUILDING

A - DR. HEATH'S LABORATORY
B - SECRET LABORATORY
C - OBSERVATION CENTER
D - INNER OFFICE
E - SECRETARY'S OFFICE
F - CLOSETS

1 - SAFE
2 - CLOCK
3 - CAMERA RANGE
4 - INFRARED RECEIVER
5 - TV CAMERA
6 - ENTRANCE
7 - TV CONSOLE
8 - LOCKERS
9 - VIDEO TAPE MACHINES

the two inside microfilmed the material and flew it out in a model airplane. I saw a spy do that once on the tube. Or they could have simply hidden the papers. All I know is that those two watching the television screen have to be guilty! That idle prattle of the one that he's a 'Christian' and 'born again' is pure balderdash! They're knaves, both of them!"

At this point Geoffrey interceded—noting the livid anger of his guest.

"Now, Heath, you're going to have to calm down. That simply won't do. Have another sip of tea and get a grip on yourself."

"Yes, yes. I'll do that."

The scientist took a deep breath and forced himself to relax. Slowly the flush left his cheeks, and his color returned to normal. Only the nervous drumming of fingers betrayed his lingering agitation. He forced down a swallow of tea and looked hopefully at my colleague.

"Mr. Weston, can you shed any light on our mystery?"

"I'm afraid," Geoffrey explained, "it's not as simple as that. This is a matter which will require a thorough investigation."

"But you *will* take the case?"

"Oh, very definitely yes. I wouldn't miss it for the world." Geoffrey now addressed the Inspector. "Twigg, have you learned anything from the guards?"

"No, we haven't. The two in the communications center claim that they watched the screens every minute and saw nothing. The three outside agree. No one entered. No one left. The lights never flickered."

"Did they have dogs?"

"No, Weston, they did not. Their dog died this week. It seems he went mad and had to be shot."

"A new one," Arthur added, "will arrive tomorrow.

There was a delay in finding a suitable replacement. Watchdogs are not easy to acquire—the crime rate being what it is. They're very much in demand."

"I'm sure they are," Geoffrey agreed. He continued his conversation with the Inspector.

"Don't you think it suggestive, Twigg, that there was no dog?"

"Only if our thief were invisible but had halitosis."

"Precisely."

"You've got to be joking."

"Perhaps, Twigg, but I would recommend that an autopsy be performed on that dog."

"If you wish, we'll do it. But I doubt you'll find any poison."

"We may not. But we *will* find out why the dog died. Have all the guards agreed to a polygraph test?"

"Yes, they have. We expect to get started on that at about three this afternoon. But, frankly, I don't think much will come of it. The men seem as puzzled as we are. And their records are flawless. The man with whom Dr. Heath seems particularly miffed has been with Metropol for twenty years."

Geoffrey looked sternly at Heath.

"Doctor, can you tell me the nature of the papers which were stolen from the safe?"

"No. I'm afraid not."

"The knowledge may be critical to the investigation."

"I can," Heath repeated, "reveal nothing. The information is classified."

"Can you tell me then, in general terms, the nature of your laboratory's research?"

"Not even that."

"But if those who wanted it already have the material, why continue to keep it a secret?"

"I'm sure I'm not at liberty to say."

"Very well," Weston sighed. "Then you've given me all the information that I can expect. It may not be enough. If you would be so good as to scribble down a few directions to get us there, we'll stop by the laboratory at six o'clock this afternoon."

Without waiting for a reply, Geoffrey shifted his gaze to the Inspector.

"I presume, Twigg, that the grounds have been sealed off."

"Yes, they have, Weston. But can't you come any sooner?"

"No. I want to arrive at a time when I can have a look around in the daylight but finish up after dark when lighting conditions duplicate those at the time of the theft. I would also like to have the polygraph results in hand before visiting the scene of the crime. I do have one request, however. Please send over some photos of the room and of the corridor—along with paint samples from the walls."

"When," the Inspector asked, "do you need the information?"

"Within the hour, if possible."

"I'll see what I can do." Twigg put down his teacup. "Dr. Heath, you no doubt have some other things you'd like to be doing. And I want to get on with questioning the staff."

Inspector Twigg rose to his feet. Following suit, the three of us stood. Our meeting was at an end. Arthur Heath handed Geoffrey a map that he had been sketching. I accompanied our two visitors as far as the sidewalk. In a moment their motorcar careened down the street, turned onto Marylebone Road, and disappeared from view.

I stood for a while, leaning against a lamp post and

admiring the morning. The air seemed cleaner than it had been in years. It was actually refreshing! This was my home, and I loved it—from the uneven, wide sidewalks to the three-story brownstones that were as solid and ugly now as they had been in Victoria's day. I waved at a passing bicyclist, took one last deep breath of fresh air, and somewhat regretfully retraced my steps to our quarters.

When I entered the living room I found my colleague seated, munching Spanish peanuts, and staring into space. It did not take a detective to know he was asking himself the question: "If I were the thief, how would I have pulled off the robbery?" I commented on the obvious.

"Ah, I see the theft has caught your fancy. What do you make of it?"

"John," Weston replied, "it's not just the theft. It's everything connected with the case. We have a triple mystery here. How were the papers stolen? Why was the dog shot? And why won't Dr. Heath even give a general accounting of the laboratory's activities? Surely he has nothing to lose, now that the papers are out— unless . . . I have a feeling, Taylor, that we won't answer the question of the disappearance until we've solved the related mysteries."

"But surely the dog was shot because he had rabies."

"I hardly think so. A watchdog is too valuable an animal not to be innoculated regularly. And it's just too much of a coincidence that the dog died within days of the robbery. One almost wonders whether the laboratory produced something that escaped into the air and affected the dog—motivating some repentant scientist to steal the papers to stop the research. The presence of poisons would certainly explain why Dr. Heath does not want news of what he is doing to get out. The citizens of Dorking would storm the buildings en masse. But somehow I think it's more likely the dog was intentionally killed. Poisons may be specific to certain species, but I doubt that one could drive an animal insane without having *any* effect at all upon humans. What was your impression of the good doctor?"

"Frankly," I admitted, "he is not my cup of tea. He strikes me as being too much the bureaucrat."

"He was rather defensive," Geoffrey agreed. "I think that attack on the guards was to divert suspicion from himself."

"Then you believe he may—"

"I don't know. The fellow may just be insecure in his job. Or he may be on the ragged edge. I'm afraid I'm a better judge of physical evidence than of people."

"I wouldn't say that," I disagreed. "It simply takes more time to know a person."

"And time," Weston commented dourly, "is something we don't have. Sometimes when we talk to suspects and witnesses, I feel rather like King Charles reviewing the troops. There's just line after line of nameless faces and faceless names. The sad part of it is that knowing a chap's personality can be fully as much a clue as finding a fingerprint."

"We live in the age of the specialist," I pointed out. "I guess we're a product of that. How could we be anything else—the population being what it is. Even the churches are largely impersonal. Evangelists move about preaching to strangers—and using wireless and the tube."

"But how much more effective would they be," Geoffrey wondered aloud, "if they preached the gospel to people that they knew? John, let's start off right on this case. Let's follow the evangelists' example and talk to Someone who understands human beings."

We bowed our heads. As was our custom, I took the lead in prayer.

"Father, only you can see the human heart. But as we make our investigation, we ask you to give us a glimpse now and then. When Achan stole silver coins and a bar of gold, you led Joshua, the first detective, to him. We ask your guidance as we investigate this affair at Pinehurst. Above all, we ask in Jesus' name that your will be done. Amen."

I now thumbed through record albums, selected a disc, put it on the turntable, and sat down. Soon we were basking in the ebb and flow of Dvorak's *Slawische Tanze* as interpreted by Herbert Von Karajan and the Berlin Philharmonic. It was a collector's item—and one of our favorites. While we listened, Geoffrey took a Bible from the table beside his chair and turned to the Psalms. In a matter of moments his hawkish intensity faded into peacefulness. He was putting the action and danger of the days ahead into their proper perspective.

As the second side of the record was nearing an end, the screech of tires announced the arrival of our bundle. The officer was about to knock on the door as I opened it and relieved him of his burden.

"Thank you very much, Whitney. Tell the Inspector that we appreciate his prompt action." Whitney was a smallish man and starched to the toes. His voice was as formal as his uniform.

"Yes, indeed, sir. Good day, sir."

"And good day to you," I replied.

I closed the door and returned to the living room—opening the packet as I walked. The Inspector, as usual, had done his job in a thoroughly professional manner. As I leafed through papers, I commented to Weston on the contents.

"Hum . . . Here's the information on the paint. The

hall appears to have been done in a 'robin's egg' blue. One wonders if the robins were consulted. The laboratory walls are, of all things, a 'powder puff' pink. Not very sedate for a research institution, if you ask me!"

"It's not all that easy," Geoffrey observed somewhat dryly, "to color coordinate for Petri dishes and Bunsen burners. At least pastels have the advantage of helping to keep the scientists awake.

"And," I observed, "no doubt the reason for that is the animated conversation by the workers on the bad taste of whoever chose the colors."

"You're too stuffy and traditional, old boy."

"And you're too avant-garde. I'll never forget the time you walked into the apartment wearing that hideous purple and florescent-green pin stripe!"

"Ah, yes." Geoffrey smiled at the memory. "It was worth it all just to see your expression! I don't believe I've ever seen you look quite so ill. What do you think of the cashmere pull-over I'm wearing now?"

"Do you really want to know?"

"No, I don't suppose I do. Let me have a look at Twigg's photographs, will you?" I handed him the stack of eight-by-ten glossies. As I peered over his shoulder, he sifted through the pile. Geoffrey was obviously enjoying himself. He stopped at a picture of the corridor directly outside the room containing the safe. His fist came hard on the arm of the chair. "That's it, John. It has to be. Have a look at the camera in the corner. Notice that it's aimed down the corridor—away from the laboratory. The laboratory door can't possibly be in its field of vision. And a bulb near the end of the hall has burned out—casting dark shadows over there. Now let's have a look at what's on the other side of that door." He shuffled through the prints until he found several of that room. After a moment of careful study, he nodded his head.

"Just as I suspected! The camera in this room is mounted almost back to back with the one in the hall—and at about the same angle. Again, the door is in a blind spot. And so is the entire wall to its right. If a fellow managed to make it from the shadows to the door area without being seen, he could open the door without any risk and slide along that right wall to within a couple of feet of the safe."

"But those last couple of feet," I pointed out, "are impossible. And what about the infrared light beam in the corridor?"

"Actually," Weston corrected, "there are two of them. The first is about two feet high, and the second a couple of feet directly above it. And they're in full view of the hall camera."

"It's wonderful," I commented dryly, "how you've simplified matters. All the thief had to do was run up twenty feet of brightly lighted, televised corridor, high-jumping a light beam on the way. Once in the laboratory his only minor problem was to walk two feet into camera range without being seen, stick his ear to the safe, and open it up."

"You could put it that way," Weston grinned. "But let's give him the option of coming in the back door in full view of the laboratory camera."

"I meant to ask about that. Why didn't Twigg say anything about a door in the rear wall?"

"Probably because we didn't ask," Geoffrey chuckled. "But seriously, with a transom over it like that, it's not a closet. And the Inspector would have mentioned it if it were anything but a dead end. It may be some sort of inner research center without windows or doors—other than that one, of course."

"So," I moaned, "we're back to our Olympic high-jumper."

"I have a theory," Geoffrey confided.

"I thought you would."

"This evening we'll have an opportunity to test it out. But first we'll need to buy some paint, paper, and lumber. And there's an artist in the West End whom I rendered a small service once that we'll have to—"

With a loud crack one of the window panes exploded inward, scattering glass into the living room. Instinctively, both of us dove to the floor.

"Somebody's shooting at us, Weston!" I shouted. "Where's my Webley?" I crawled over to the desk and started opening drawers. "It's got to be around here somewhere!"

"I've found it, John," Geoffrey half whispered from across the room. "Hold tight. I'll be back in a moment." He rushed the front door, slammed it open, and ran crouching into the street. I expected to hear shots, but there were none. After what seemed an eternity, he strode back through the doorway.

"Whoever it was," he declared, "was devilishly quick. He was gone by the time I reached the street. I didn't catch so much as a glimpse."

"It's fortunate for us," I observed, "that he was a bad shot."

Weston smiled. "I don't know about that, old boy. There's a scratch on the edge of one of the fence posts outside. The bullet must have been deflected. Be a good chap and find the slug while I have a talk with the police. Oh yes, you might also close the drapes on the off chance of our visitor's return." He walked over to the telephone table and hastily punched out the number on the dial.

"Hello. This is Geoffrey Weston here. I'd like to

speak with Inspector Twigg, please . . . Well, could you patch me through to him? Thank you . . . Twigg, this is Weston. Somebody's just taken a shot at us over here. Would you please run and check on the Pinehurst employees and their families? Let me know if anyone's missing . . . Certainly I think one of them might have done it. Who knows we're on the case? Everyone! Well, that certainly narrows things down. Somebody over there must have given us a pretty big build up."

I handed Geoffrey the slug that I'd dug out of the wall next to the fireplace. It was bent almost flat.

"And Twigg," he continued, "check to see if any of them owns a seven millimeter rifle . . . No, I didn't happen to notice the make. Of course I'd like you to patrol the area. Call me back in an hour or two with what you've got. Thank you . . . The same to you." He hung up the phone.

A half hour later our station wagon was wending its way across town toward the West End. The luggage space was piled high with paint cans, cardboard, strips of wood, tacks, screws, and "L" stands—plus, of course, a pane of glass that we'd purchased for the window. Geoffrey had seemingly put the mystery out of his mind. As he steered, he gave me a different kind of tour of the city.

"Look over there, Taylor. What do you see?" He pointed with his index finger as we whipped around a turn. I twisted my neck to get a glimpse.

"A . . . moderately ugly building. Why?"

"Precisely. But why do we see that kind of building? We see it because what purports to be civilized progress is a fraud. There was once a mediaeval church on that site. It was a work of art—with flying buttresses, stained glass windows, and the lot. The choir and steeple perished in the Great Fire. But it took our modern civilized world to administer the coup de grâce."

"How did it happen?"

"A direct hit during the war. Now it's been replaced by that monstrosity! Progress . . . It's the destruction of our roots to make way for more cracker-box houses!"

"But surely, Weston, man will produce other architectural gems."

"Yes. And he will destroy them. Cement, steel, and the assembly line are replacing the work of the artisan. I tell you, we are only a stone's throw from assembly line people! I think our artists, architects, and musicians go to school today to learn how to make twenty-first century gargoyles. Did you hear about that composer who wrote an entire symphony with random notes? When he finished conducting the first performance, his own musicians hissed him. And I'm hissing, too. What a slap in the face of reason, order, and real talent! Our civilization is decaying, John. You and I are simply repairmen who put together a few fractured pieces. Without us the disintegration would be a little faster, that's all."

Geoffrey and I rode on in silence. There was no point in answering his charges. And, frankly, I'm not sure that I could. It often seemed to me, as well, that the detective might be the last holdout for order and absolute ethics in a world gone mad.

Now nearing the West End, we turned onto Piccadilly. Geoffrey picked up the thread of our conversation as though there had been no pause.

"That's what I mean, John. Look over there. That used to be the Turf Club—built centuries ago to be a duke's mansion. They blew it up in the 1960's to build what you see now. And over there . . ." He gestured to our left. "Can anyone really be satisfied with Stratton House, knowing what it replaced? Where is Devonshire House? It makes me sick to think of a steel ball demolishing the marble staircases and sculptured ceilings. They murdered that house, John. I can think of no better term for it. They murdered what older hands than theirs had toiled to give elegance. They robbed us of a part of our past. And it wasn't Germans, either! Englishmen planted the charges. Englishmen manned the machines." He looked now toward a side street a bit ahead of us and to the right. "Down Arlington Street there, they knocked out everything on the right side. THEY, John, THEY—the unidentifiable, faceless horde that escapes without being noticed or condemned! They're men following orders by men following orders by men who have taken a poll. The streets of London are a graveyard of old houses. We've adopted America's mania for change."

Within a short while we sped around a corner, escaping Piccadilly and braking to a halt three blocks down the street in front of a ramshackle brick structure. From its appearance, I would say that it had begun its career as a warehouse. Now it was an apartment building. Weston commented with a note of sarcasm that at least it was still there. I waited in the motorcar while he went to one of the front doors. We did not particularly wish to leave our Mercedes unattended in that neighborhood. He soon returned, and I helped unload. Together, we carried a portion of our booty up the steps and into what would normally have been a living room. I looked about in amazement.

"Why, Weston, I never would have believed it. The room appears to have reverted back into a warehouse."

"It does rather seem so," my friend agreed. "Which only goes to prove that an artist has greater opportunity for sloppiness than does a detective."

"And creative sloppiness, at that! But where's the artist? Is he hiding somewhere in that forest of frames, nursery school faces, and canvas?"

Geoffrey's voice dropped to little more than a whisper. "Not so loudly, John, or you'll offend him!" He now spoke normally. "I'm afraid we've caught our host in the middle of taking a shower. He told me through the door to drop off the materials, pictures, and a rough sketch of what we want. I've already drawn a sketch. And, fortunately, one of Twigg's men made a notation of the dimensions of the safe. So Tom here will be able to paint to scale without much bother." I now noticed the sound of running water coming from another room. I waited until we went outside for the second load before mentioning the man's paintings again.

"How can he produce that kind of drivel and still pay the rent?"

Geoffrey opened the rear of the station wagon and hefted a couple of cans of paint. He paused to look at me thoughtfully. "He can't, John. It's his jobs for people like us that keep the wolf from his door. He's trying to find himself. That's his cubist phase—order but no beauty. Tom says he's looking for the ideal behind the particular."

"And so," I concluded, "he butchers the particular."

"I've told him that there is only one ideal. But to him Jesus is merely an object to be painted. And when he paints Christ, he distorts. He needs our understanding and friendship—and our prayers." As he spoke we finished loading up and began carrying the last of the assortment toward the building. I had only one objection to what he had said.

"Weston, friendship and prayer I can supply. But I doubt that I'll ever understand the man. You were thinking of him when you gave me the guided tour, weren't you?"

My colleague responded with a chuckle as we were nearing the steps.

"You should have seen his work while he was in his neo-Dada, tachist, and pop art phases! He's been progressing toward the real world. Now that he's a cubist, I call him 'square.' He doesn't like that."

We dropped the last of the supplies off in the apartment and began our drive back to Baker Street. The artist had agreed to deliver the finished work to us. And Geoffrey wanted to be back in our quarters to receive Twigg's call. We threaded our way through traffic and arrived home at a little before three. We had a bite to eat and waited. At three-thirty the phone rang. Weston, who was sitting in his reading chair, picked up the receiver.

"Hello. Yes, I was expecting you, Twigg. For everyone else I let it ring a second time. How did it go? . . . You don't say. What about the polygraph tests? About what we thought . . . Yes. I'd like them on duty this evening if you could arrange it. Wonderful! I'll see you later. Cheerio."

Geoffrey returned the receiver to its hook, closed his eyes, and leaned back in the recliner. I waited for him to give me a report. But with a hot meal in him and nothing to do but wait for the artist's delivery, it wasn't long before he began to snore. At first his attempts were feeble, but they gradually increased in volume into regular bull bellows. It's a wonder he didn't wake himself up! I sent thanksgiving heavenward that my bedroom is so nearly soundproof. Only thick walls and its location at the other end of the hall from Geoffrey's room had spared me from certain insomnia.

For my friend's sake, I moved about the room as

quietly as possible. For the next several days we were both likely to be rather short on sleep. I replaced the broken pane. Then, choosing a book on chess tactics from the case by the mantle, I set about improving my mind. It was difficult, however, to concentrate. I was immensely curious as to what Twigg had said.

At four-thirty an ancient van rattled to a stop out front. I opened the curtains a crack and got an eyeful. From bumper to bumper it was covered with paintings of flowers and birds, and of things that go bump in the night. Featured on the side were the heads of two people who looked as though they had been trapped in a trash compacter. Our artist had obviously arrived. I met him on the sidewalk and helped him transfer his completed project into the station wagon. He'd wrapped the lot in brown paper.

Tom Rainwater was a small, thin-boned man with constantly moving eyes. He more fitted my concept of a pickpocket than of a painter. But there was no denying his talent—at least when he followed other people's instructions rather than his own inclinations. The two or three times he'd done work for us, we hadn't been disappointed.

When I returned to our lodgings, I found Weston already awake. He had extracted a box about the size of a salt shaker from one of the drawers of the work bench. He had obviously seen Tom and myself through the window as we loaded up the car. As Geoffrey walked toward the door, his hand fished his coat from off the sofa.

"Well, John, we'd best get to work. There's a thief to catch. Grab your briefcase and we'll be off."

I obliged.

CHAPTER 2

Experiment at Dorking

We once again drove down Baker Street—this time taking a turn onto Marylebone and then another to the southwest. A short time later we passed out of the city limits and were within about fifteen kilometers of Dorking. As the traffic eased, Geoffrey relaxed a bit and we began to enjoy the scenery. The odors of London thinned. The nip of frosty air was bracing. Russet, brown, and yellow leaves decked the trees, blanketed the countryside, and now and then encroached in drifts upon the roadway. I took a deep breath and stretched limbs that had been confined to a motorcar or a chair for too much of the day.

"Now there," I declared with appreciation, "is a *real* work of art."

"Indeed it is," Geoffrey agreed. "It has everything— balance, symmetry, color, and pools of sunlight in just the right places."

We drove on for a while—savoring the sight. All the time I wondered when my partner would let me know what he had learned from the Inspector. Finally, I could stand the suspense no longer.

"Weston," I asked abruptly, "what on earth did Twigg say? I've been dying of curiosity. Does he have any idea who shot at us?"

"I'm sorry, old chap," he answered sheepishly. "I wasn't thinking. Actually, Twigg was as much in the dark as we are. Everyone had an alibi of sorts. And as I'd expected, the polygraph tests were negative. You'd hardly expect a man to agree to them, after all, unless he thought he'd pass."

I had been—from time to time—glancing at the map that Dr. Heath had left with us. We were nearing a crossroad.

"There's the sign." I gestured toward the intersection. "Take a right turn here."

Moments later we came to a stop at the front gate of Pinehurst Laboratory. The guard, as well as a representative of the Yard, examined our papers and allowed us to pass.

The laboratory buildings were arranged into two neat rows separated by the entrance road. The longer structure was on the right and the two shorter ones were to the left. The whole affair had a drab military appearance—perhaps bespeaking its former use. Asphalt widened at the complex to completely cover the ground between the buildings. We'd get no footprints or tire impressions here—though no motorcar could have entered unseen anyway. For that matter, neither could a man.

Twigg was awaiting us at the doorway of the building on the left. Geoffrey pulled the station wagon over and stopped almost directly in front of the Inspector—turning to face him through the window.

"Good to see you, Twigg. Have you had any difficulty with the guards? They're all here, I hope."

Twigg answered with a twinkle in his eye.

"You've no worry there, Weston. Your problem's going to be finding the little invisible man who came and went and snatched papers through three inches of solid steel without leaving a dent in the safe."

"Well, if that's my problem, what say we get on with the solution. I presume that this is the building where the theft took place."

"It is."

I retrieved my briefcase from the back seat of the Mercedes, and we approached the structure almost warily—as though it were a foe to be mastered. The place had the air of a mausoleum. Not so much as a window interrupted the starkness of painted cement. Recessed double doors alone reminded us that this was indeed a laboratory and not a giant slab of stone. We walked the few feet to those doors—the front entrance. Geoffrey took the magnifying glass from his pocket and began a careful examination. As he did so, he shot a question at Twigg.

"May I assume that these doors were locked last night?"

"You may, indeed. Dr. Heath remembers specifically that he had to use his key to get in. And a guard on outdoor rounds found them secured an hour earlier."

"And what of the rear entrance?"

"There is none," Twigg informed him.

"Not even a fire exit?"

"What you see in front is what you see in back—minus the opening."

Geoffrey seemed genuinely surprised. He stepped back from the facade and surveyed the blank exterior from end to end.

"Twigg," he observed, "if you look closely you can see the outlines of windows that have been bricked in. I presume, therefore, that the odd nature of the building is not a legacy from the military. How do you suppose the Pinehurst people managed to break so many safety regulations and get away with it?"

The Inspector shrugged his shoulders.

"There are some places, you know, that don't have to count their fire escapes. Prisons, for example. . ."

"Are government owned," Geoffrey concluded. "Authorities are notoriously quick at giving themselves exemptions. But how does a private company go about cutting red tape? And why would they want to do it, anyway? What are they hiding?"

"That," the Inspector declared rather stiffly, "is none of my concern. Cement is not particularly apt to burn, and a single entrance simplifies security. Must I remind you that you and Taylor are here to investigate a theft—not your client?"

"I'll try to remember that," Weston replied dryly. "I don't suppose there are any skylights?"

"No."

"I didn't think so. What about trap doors and tunnels?"

"There are none. We've taken soundings. And the sewer pipes are too small to accommodate even a child."

"Then," Weston noted with a touch of banter, "we seem to be suffering from simplicity."

"That's the devil of it," Twigg agreed. "If you look at the two corners of the laboratory across the way—at just about roof level—you'll see cameras trained down on us. There is only one entrance to the building where the theft occurred. No one can enter without being seen. Once inside, there is only one passageway to the room containing the safe. Nobody can pass through it without being observed. Inside the room, there is one safe with one door being viewed by one camera. What we have here are a series of simple impossibilities! Not even a ghost could have pulled it off! We would have seen the safe open."

Geoffrey's voice betrayed his sympathy.

"You'll grant, though, that the front doors are indented just far enough into the wall to hide anyone reaching that recess from exposure by the cameras."

"You're a big help," Twigg complained. "Shall we teleport our criminal to the vestibule?"

"My word, Twigg, you've got imagination. There's hope for you yet."

A dour glance from the Inspector, however, indicated that he did not take his own suggestion seriously. Geoffrey recognized the impasse in the conversation and once again approached the massive oaken doors with his lens. He paid particular attention to the area around the lock.

"There is," Twigg commented helpfully, "no evidence of tampering. As you can see, there are no scratches on either the metal or the wood. But then a door would hardly pose a problem to a man who can enter a safe without opening it."

"Indeed it wouldn't," Geoffrey agreed. "One of these days you're going to make a sarcastic remark that solves a case by mistake. What about the laboratory in question? Where is the room?"

"I'll take you there," Twigg offered.

"No. John and I would prefer to make our investigation alone, if you don't mind. I rather feel like a typist with someone looking over his shoulder. Nothing personal, Inspector, but your standing there like that makes me a trifle self-conscious." So saying, Geoffrey got up off his knees, slid the glass into his pocket, and turned to face the Inspector—who had indeed been peering over my companion's shoulder at his examination of the lock.

"Sorry, old chap," the Scotland Yarder replied in a tone which implied he wasn't. "I had no idea you were so sensitive."

"A sensitive instrument," I interjected in defense of Weston, "is most necessary for detecting minute but significant clues."

"Well said," Twigg replied. "You've been reading the backs of cereal boxes again. If you two 'crimometers' will walk through the door, down the hall, take the first right and the following left, you should find yourselves at the entrance to the laboratory—that is, unless you get lost."

"We will do our best," Geoffrey assured him, "to avoid becoming missing persons."

"Twigg," I asked, "what is the word on fingerprints? I presume you've dusted the usual places—doors, the piece of paper, the face of the safe?"

"Not only that, Taylor. We've checked every piece of glass in the laboratory. We've checked the inside of the safe. We've even dusted the posts and crossbars of the fence that surrounds the complex."

"And you've found?" I inquired.

"Nothing."

"What about that back room behind the laboratory?"

"I'm afraid I haven't seen it," the Inspector admitted. "The area is classified. But I've gotten a peek at the building plans. The room is a dead end. It is, of course, windowless. The only door is the entrance from Heath's laboratory. And heating ducts are far too small to admit man or monkey. Unless our thief was a trained cat, he could have neither entered nor escaped by that route.

"Don't try to go in that back room or you'll have the guards down on you in a minute. That reminds me . . . If you two gentlemen are determined to conduct your investigation alone, I had best stroll on down to the guards' office and tell the men on duty to expect you on their screens. Otherwise, you'll have a good bit more company than you have right now."

"Thank you, Inspector, " I replied. "We appreciate your efforts."

Twigg and I shook hands, and he turned and walked down the hall with his usual crisp step. It was anything but a stroll. While the two of us had been talking, Geoffrey had gone to his hands and knees just inside the entrance. He was minutely inspecting the floor with his lens. Now that the Scotland Yarder was gone, Weston—without looking up from his task—gave me my instructions.

"John, come on behind me, will you? Take a close look at the walls and see whether or not there are any new scratches. I would expect them to be at the turns, but you never know. They could be anywhere."

Foot by foot he crisscrossed the corridor—slowly advancing in the direction of the laboratory. I followed with magnifier in hand. The paint on the walls was almost new. I examined every inch of it, hoping to find surface scratches. All I discovered, however, was that the painter had been in a hurry. In places cement showed through. In others, lines wiggled or paint dripped. In short, I found a commentary on the times but none on the crime.

We turned the corner and worked our way to the right until we reached the corridor leading off to the left. The laboratory was at the end of that hall. My own searches still had shown nothing. Weston had stopped twice to examine faint marks on the floor.

The light at the junction—the bulb that we had noticed in the photographs—was still out. Since visibility was too poor at that point to permit close inspection, we by-passed the area and walked up that final corridor into view of the television camera.

"I say, Weston," I remarked, "now you've got Twigg peering over your shoulder again via the 'tele.' "

"You can depend on that," Geoffrey agreed. "But at least I can't feel him breathing on the back of my neck. Have a look, will you, at the area of wall around the infrared receiving units? If I'm correct, there just may be some traces of glue clinging to the paint."

Weston got down on his hands and knees once again. His nose almost to the floor, he began casting about like a bloodhound in search of the scent. I bent over and closely examined both receivers. Neither had even a modicum of glue anywhere near it. But there were some rather curious, minute scratches on the surface around the devices.

"This is most odd," I mumbled to no one in particular. "If there was any glue, I fancy that it has been removed with sandpaper. But that makes no sense at all. Why not just use rubber cement to begin with and then rub it off?"

My companion got to his feet and came over.

"Let me have a look at that."

He knelt and carefully scrutinized the area. His lens now and again stopped as he found abrasions.

"John," he observed, "odd is not the word for it. This is downright singular. If you'll notice, there is even a slight surface scratch on one of the receiving lenses. And I have not found the faint scuff marks which I had expected to be on the floor along the right wall. There are, however, two slight half-moon scrapes in the wax in the middle of the floor. They are nearly identical to marks just inside the entrance to the building. In each instance the half-moon seems to be aiming at the laboratory door—the apex of the arc nearer the laboratory and digging just a slight bit deeper into the wax. Then there's this . . . " He handed me an envelope. "I'll want you to make some tests on the contents when we're back at Baker Street."

I looked inside and found what seemed to be a glass bead. It was somewhat smaller than a grain of sand.

"Could this," I speculated, "be what scratched the receiver?"

Geoffrey's eyes sparkled as he answered.

"I'm virtually certain of it, old boy. But the question is, what does it all mean? Things are getting more interesting by the minute. I'm beginning to think that my method for entering the laboratory is altogether too simple. But when we finish inspecting the room, let's have some fun anyway."

We moved on to the door at the end of the hall. The lock was of the very best manufacture. There was no sign of tampering. The jam folded around the door so that no thin object could be inserted to slip the latch. Nor could we find evidence that anything had been placed there before the door was closed to keep it from locking.

The laboratory itself was unimpressive. A Bunsen burner, some test tubes, and a pipette were in view. Otherwise the tables to the left were empty. The mysterious backdoor was the main attraction. But with the guards' eyes staring down upon us, we were not about to seem inquisitive. After a methodical search, all we had come up with were two grey hairs which probably belonged to Dr. Heath. Heating ducts were small. Gratings were securely fastened. The safe was of modern design and not a kind that could be easily cracked. Its inner walls were as solid as a rock and normal in every way. No doubt Twigg had found the wall behind the safe to be undisturbed.

Weston dropped the magnifying glass back into his pocket, closed the safe, and shrugged.

"Well, there's nothing more we can do here," he declared. "Let's try to find the Inspector. On the way, I'll give you instructions as to what to do with the equipment in the car."

As we walked down the corridors, my partner filled me in on his plan. We almost bumped into Twigg at the second turn. He was coming to meet us. Geoffrey spoke first.

"Ah, Twigg! You're just the sapling we've been looking for. We'd as leaf have Twigg as any tree in the forest."

A groan escaped the lips of our distinguished friend.

"Just remember," he replied, "that it was a single twig that broke the camel's back."

"Well, well," Weston shot back, "what's a Twigg without bark! How's your bite?"

Double groan! When those two get started, there's very little that a sane soul can do but to escape. I could see it coming: "My but the Twiggy look has changed! A little broad of beam for a Twigg, aren't you? How many nuts are in your family, Twigg?" "There's a hot wind blowing from the Weston." "Don't be snappy, Twigg . . ." etc., ad nauseam. I interrupted before they got up a head of steam.

"Excuse me, fellows, but I have some work to do in the car. And, Inspector, Geoffrey would like you to take him by the guards' office so he can have a look at the equipment and chat with the gentlemen who were on duty last night."

As I walked away, the two patted each other on the back and went around the corner—laughing heartily. I stepped outside and began gathering up the various bundles from the back of the station wagon. I cannot, therefore, give a firsthand account of what happened in the observation center. But from talking with Geoffrey afterwards, I can pretty well reconstruct the events—even to some of the dialogue.

The two were still chuckling as they entered the center. Weston then made a thorough inspection of the videotape equipment—asking the guards occasional questions as to its use and limitations. The security men sat in swivel chairs before the console. Every now and then they took their eyes off the bank of screens to glance in his direction. There was still classified information lying about the laboratories, and they were not about to let any more of it get away. The older guard was Tom Yancy. He looked to be about retirement age, but he was still rugged. The younger, Earl Garfield, was of medium height and build. He was the more talkative of the two.

Weston, his survey of the gadgetry now completed, pulled up a chair and got down to serious questioning. He met the guards' glances with a steady gaze.

"Did either of you," he prompted, "notice anything out of the ordinary last night? Anything at all—no matter how insignificant it might seem?"

"There wasn't nothin' what 'appened 'ere," Earl Garfield volunteered. "Me and Pop 'ardly could keep our eyes open, it was so boring—that is until 'eath walked in with 'is blinkin' insomnia."

The older guard, however, did not agree.

"Now that's not quite true, Earl. You remember I told you a little after midnight that I had a feeling something was wrong. It was like a cloud was hovering just past the edge of my vision. I had the impression that I was being stalked by something malign."

"I remember it rightly enough," Garfield chided. "That foolishness was all what kept me awake. It like to

put chills down my spine, comin' at that time o' night."
He now addressed Geoffrey. "You'll 'ave to 'scuse Tom,
Mister Weston. 'e's a bit odd—some sort o' religious
fanatic."

Weston gazed past Garfield toward the top shelf of
an open locker. His response was a trifle sarcastic.

"Strange, Earl, that you should say that about your
partner. From the looks of those paperbacks and
magazines over there, I should have taken you for the
religious one."

Puzzlement and surprise both showed upon the
guard's face.

" 'ow'd you know they was mine? And what's that
got t' do wi' the price o' fish?"

"Why," Geoffrey explained with a gesture toward
the locker, "that clothing over there could hardly be
your partner's. It's three sizes too small. And the other
guards would have locked up before leaving. That leaves
you as the worshipper of Bacchus."

"The what o' what?"

"Oh come now, good fellow," Weston explained in
his best pedantic manner, "the word is spelled B-A-C-C-
H-U-S. You'll find it in the dictionary. Look it up. It
will do you good to read something that isn't filled with
pictures of naked women."

"Now look 'ere!" Garfield protested.

"You'd better do the looking yourself, young
fellow." Geoffrey pointed to one of the screens on the
console. "What's that on the tube?"

At the very instant that Weston spoke, both Twigg
and Yancy let out a yell. In front of their eyes, a certain
John Taylor, Esq., had jumped out of the door to the
safe and was making faces at them. It was my debut, and
I fear I made the most of it. Twigg, who had remained in

the background during the questioning, was thunderstruck.

"How'd he do it, Weston!" he wanted to know. "How'd he get in there?"

"I thought you might like to know," Geoffrey replied. "If you gentlemen will accompany me to the laboratory, I think your curiosity will be satisfied."

The two guards and the detective fairly stormed the door to get out of the office and on their way down the hall. Weston followed at a more leisurely pace. Meanwhile, I left the laboratory and walked into the corridor to greet what I felt certain would be a very agitated committee. Twigg was the first to arrive—puffing and somewhat redder in the face than usual. He took one look at the equipment I had assembled and shot a question at me.

"What's that stuff there? What did you do?"

"Let's wait until the others arrive," I demurred. "This is Geoffrey's show."

In a matter of seconds Yancy and Garfield arrived neck and neck. They followed Twigg's example by rumbling to a stop and staring at the object that my partner had contrived with the aid of the artist. Geoffrey turned the corner and strolled toward us humming the Marseillaise.

"Well, gentlemen," he addressed the group, "what do you think of our little surprise?"

Twigg was the first to speak.

"How does it work, Weston? Why didn't we see it?"

"You didn't see it," Geoffrey assured him, "because it was invisible."

"Preposterous!"

"No, not at all," he explained to the Scotland Yarder. "What you see by the wall is, even now, still invisible on the television screens. The principle is an old one. I've simply borrowed a trick from the chameleon. As you know, television cameras do not have depth perception. No matter how sharp the focus, they cannot distinguish between two objects of identical color if their outlines merge."

We walked over to the contraption and began pointing out its features.

"You will notice," he continued, "that this is nothing more than three strips of cardboard. Each segment is nine foot long and three foot high. They are so put together that they telescope outward to a length of twenty-five feet. The apparatus is, of course, painted the exact shade of blue as the wall behind it. Its folding legs can be seen from the rear only. Each cardboard segment has a hook attached so that it can be extended by that pole over there." He gestured toward an aluminum rod lying on the floor nearby. "The end of the pole also fits a hole on the side of that blue tube glued to the wall. Now, John, will you explain to us how you eluded the television camera and the light beam?"

"Gladly." I picked up the rod and used it as a pointer. "I was back in those shadows under the burned-out bulb. From there I placed the cardboard sections flush against the wall opposite the camera and slid the main section forward into the light. It blended perfectly and was so close to the wall that it did not break the floor line. I slowly extended the second section until the notch at its end cradled the lower infrared detector. Then I angled the first section out ever so slightly from the wall. With the feet of the first section unfolded, I had a hand free to put the cardboard tube on the end of the pole. It contains a battery-powered infrared torch. I simply ran the box out on the pole behind the cardboard sections and pressed its sticky surface over the detector. Then I extended the third section to a point beyond the range of the camera and slid the sections away from the wall—gradually creating a new floor line. The movement was so slow that it went unnoticed. I crawled behind my false wall across the area covered by the camera. Once there, I opened the door and walked into the laboratory."

"And that," Weston added, "explains how our thief could have entered."

"Here, yes," Yancy agreed. "But how did he get into the building in the first place? How did he get past the gate? And how did he manage to bring in twenty-five feet of cardboard?"

"Good questions all," Geoffrey acknowledged. "How many of the cameras are tied in with videotape machines?"

"All the ones indoors," Tom replied. "When fog comes in off the moors, the outside cameras are worse than useless. So we don't bother with taping them."

"And was there fog last night?"

"Yes, Mr. Weston, there was . . . but only patches."

"And," Earl Garfield interrupted, "we're used t' that. We cou' still see everythin' as plain as day."

My partner fixed his attention upon the younger guard.

"Surely bits of fog floating in front of spotlights would cast unusual shadows. That didn't bother you?"

"Not one wit," Garfield boasted. "We've been 'ere so long that we 'ardly even notice 'em. We just looks for things what's solid. And nothin' gets by us."

"Except," Geoffrey observed, "last night." He once again turned his attention to Tom Yancy.

"Tom, I didn't see any log in your observation center. Do you keep one?"

"No. The guards at the gate take care of that."

"Wouldn't it be possible, then," Weston suggested,

"that the equipment was brought in piece by piece as the thief came to work? Then yesterday, whoever it was could have confused the log entries or have hidden an accomplice in his motorcar who didn't go home at the end of the day. Patches of fog and shadows or the confusion created by Heath's arrival might explain the escape after the crime. Or a guard at the gate might simply have let him out."

"But," Twigg reminded him, "the polygraph test—"

"Is inconclusive," Weston shot back. "What would it show if a guard had been hypnotized earlier in the week and given a post-hypnotic suggestion to sign a worker out at dusk who never left, or to allow someone to leave later on without remembering or recording the action?"

"But," Twigg objected, "surely no one can be forced to do something contrary to his conscience."

"That," Geoffrey said, "is a popular fallacy. Actually a subject can be made to do almost anything."

"I don't believe it," Twigg replied.

"Quite a few years ago—during the Second World War, I believe—the United States government proved the point rather conclusively," Weston assured him. "Hypnotized recruits were induced to attack officers by merely telling them that the officers were the Japanese enemy. Once a man's perception and motivation are manipulated, his conscience means nothing."

"Yet," the Inspector observed, "you use the words 'could' and 'might' when referring to the thief's methods. I take it that you have some doubts that he actually did what you suggest."

"Very observant of you, old fellow," Geoffrey remarked admiringly. "There are, of course, a thousand ways to peel an onion. But the same smell results. What I am doing now is proving the crime committable. The exact mechanics may be somewhat different. But the fact that we now view the theft as possible should suggest directions for further investigation."

"I don't know about you," the Scotland Yarder commented with some irritation, "but I'd like to direct this investigation through that door over there and into the laboratory. How the deuce did John jump out of that safe, anyway?" '

"John," Weston responded, "if you will lead the way . . ."

I stepped over to the door and entered the adjoining room—Twigg, Yancy, and Garfield following close at my heels. Geoffrey brought up the rear. He evidently wanted me to give the explanations.

"Once inside," I continued my monologue, "I inched along this wall to the right—taking advantage of the laboratory camera's blind spot. I walked to within three feet of the safe without being seen. You will notice that I carried something with me." Indeed, the party was noticing. Since entering the room, the two guards and the Scotland Yarder had not ceased staring at what was standing in front of the safe.

"It looks," Yancy observed, "like a stage flat."

"Or," Garfield added, "like a roll-up map—except it 'as the face o' a safe painted on it."

"Correct on both points," I agreed. "And it doesn't look particularly real to us here. But I assure you that it is much more effective when viewed from the observation center. Notice that both ends are attached to rods. I simply slid the rolled-up canvas out flush against the bottom of the safe, stood on the bottom rod, and used the other one to unroll the canvas upward. The painting exactly corresponded to the safe markings. The two feet to the right of the safe became a false wall. I then attached support brackets and a stand behind the scroll.

The whole thing was rigged so that there was a little floor-colored canvas wrapped around the bottom rod. So, as I slowly moved the prop away from the wall, I rolled up the top and unrolled the bottom just enough to maintain the floor line. As you gentlemen saw, I went behind the canvas and then sprang into camera view. It appeared as though I had jumped from the door of the safe. Our intruder, however, would have crouched behind the false front and worked the tumblers."

At this point Weston took over.

"Well, there you have it," he concluded. "The only way to have performed the robbery was for the thief to have been invisible. I have reason to doubt that he used exactly the same method that we just used, but he *must* have employed the same principle."

"Gentlemen," I noted, "I hate to bring this up. But while we've been chatting, who has been keeping watch in the observation center?"

I had literally dropped a bombshell. Yancy and Garfield looked at one another with the sickening recognition that they had abandoned their posts. My comment had been calculated to end our talk. Tom, however, was so taken up with the problem that he seemed loath to break free. We all began walking toward the hall.

"Weston," he declared somewhat weakly, "I don't suppose another minute will make much difference. And there's one more thing I want to know. What was that strange feeling I had last night.?"

"I've given some thought to that," my partner replied. "There are, of course, three possibilities. The first is that the thief's entrance caused minute changes in the television picture which triggered a reaction in your subconscious. Subliminal perception can be very disquieting. Or the whole thing may have been your imagination—the revenge of something you ate for dinner."

"You said there were three possibilities," Garfield reminded him. "What's the third?"

"Why I thought it was obvious. Perhaps," Geoffrey speculated, "an evil cloud really was hovering. Twigg, John and I have done about all we can do here today. Would you please make a copy of the videotape portion from, say, midnight to two o'clock and send it over to Baker Street sometime this evening? I'll need the view from both the hall and the laboratory. Oh yes, and I would like complete employee files and the police dossier on every worker. Tomorrow afternoon we should be ready for some interviews."

By this time our little group had reached the cross corridor that led to the outside world. With handshakes all around, we parted company with the Scotland Yarder and the two guards—who continued on their way to the observation center. In a moment Geoffrey and I had reached our motorcar and were traveling slowly along the drive.

"Keep a look out," Weston cautioned me, "for shadows. Notice the bushes. And pay particular attention to the shadows the Mercedes makes."

At the gate Geoffrey got out and made a sketch map of the grounds. He made special note of the light poles and of the areas illuminated by each bulb. While he was thus engaged, I spoke with the guard and learned that nothing out of the ordinary had happened the night before—except for the arrival of Dr. Heath and the police. According to the log, Heath had walked through the gates at exactly 1:45 a.m.

Seated once again in our station wagon, we were gently pushed backward by the acceleration. Soon Pinehurst Laboratory was left far behind. Only an occasional headlight or two coming from the other direction punctuated the darkness. And I remembered the envelope in my coat pocket.

"Do you really think," I asked, "that our thief entered in any of the ways that you suggested?"

"I would be very surprised, indeed, if he did," Geoffrey replied.

"Then why did you bring in all of those theories?"

My companion's voice was solemn.

"To keep our client out of gaol for a day or two."

We rode on in silence. The return to Baker Street was uneventful.

CHAPTER 3

Baker Street Research

Weston gazed intently into the microscope sitting before him on the table. About an hour had passed since our arrival home from Dorking, and the chill of the night air had worn off somewhat. A fire crackled warmly in the fireplace. We had just dined on fish and chips from a local carry-out shoppe. Oh, for some halibut Bristol, oxtail soup, roast pheasant, or cold woodcock! Bachelorhood has its disadvantages.

I now busied myself setting up our equipment so we would be able to view Twigg's videotapes when they arrived. Geoffrey was examining that mysterious bead that we had found in the corridor. He frowned and sat up straight.

"This is amazing, John! Come have a look."

I plugged in the last connection and stepped over to our mini-laboratory (a corner of the living room). When the microscope was focused to suit my eyes, I too was surprised.

"How strange! The entire bead seems to have dark veins running through it. It's almost as if layers of glass have been alternated with incredibly thin, black discs. Why would anyone go to all that trouble? Is it some sort of semiconductor?"

"I don't think so," Geoffrey replied. "If you turn the bead, you will notice that a movement of only a few degrees completely blocks light from passing through it. It's a bit like those traffic lights that can be seen only from the turning lane. The dark layers must serve as light channels. But as you say, why should anyone go to all the trouble? Notice the scratches on the bead where it rubbed against the wall. There are traces of glue on the opposite side. Oddly, the light channels are canted slightly at an angle."

"I'm still in the dark," I admitted. "Why were the beads scraped against the wall to begin with?"

"Let us assume," Weston replied, "that we do not have here the world's most expensive sandpaper. The beads passed in front of the detector, yet no alarm sounded. So they must have transmitted light to it. They were no doubt cemented to some sort of rear projection screen. But this particular bead was glued on at a crazy angle. Why? Since beads without the channels would transmit light to the receiver, this strange bead probably serves some purpose in that position. That purpose should become clearer as we continue to investigate. I have an idea, but it is mere speculation at this point."

"Where then," I wondered, "do we go from here?"

"There are, John, two things we might get on with. First, let's try to trace the glass—or perhaps even the beads (if they are not of private manufacture). I'll cut off a corner of the bead and run it through the spectroscope. We may find a clue to the company that made it in the composition of the glass. While I'm doing that, you might set up a tripod in front of the tube. Choose a camera with a fast lens. The screen, itself, will limit the resolution of Twigg's tapes. But I want to make at least a crude enlargement of anything interesting that we might find in them."

I went over to a cabinet and selected my favorite Japanese camera. In a moment I had it loaded and perched on a tripod in front of the television screen. I switched on the BBC, turned off a light, and set about adjusting camera settings. Meanwhile, Geoffrey was working on his project.

A short while later there was a clanging at the gate outside. I hurried to answer—expecting one of Twigg's messengers. It was, however, Arthur Heath who was standing under the street lamp.

"Well, Heath, it's you. Do come in out of the cold," I invited. "What brings you here at this late hour?"

The doctor looked terrible. He had not rested the night of the robbery, and red eyes hinted at continued sleeplessness. I ushered him into the living room and gestured toward the overstuffed chair that he had occupied that morning. He did not so much sit down as deflate. Geoffrey glanced up from his work.

"I'll be through here in a moment, Doctor. You might have a spot of tea with John while you wait."

The cup of tea is as much a part of our dealings with clients as is the chair. Heath's hand shook slightly as he took the offered cup.

"You're quite the host, Mr. Taylor. Who would have believed that tonight could be so dreary after the pleasant day we had."

"I try to make our guests comfortable," I replied. "But what brings you here, anyway?"

He sighed and spoke slowly—weighing every word.

"A combination of things, really. You may have guessed that I have hardly closed my eyes since the dreadful event. I heard about your remarkable demonstration at the laboratory, and it has caused me to do some thinking. I'm afraid that I have been so taken up with the notion that the guards are guilty that I have not been of much help. But I've gone over and over the events of the last few weeks, and I think I may have come up with something. And, well, I'm curious about what you two have been doing. I couldn't sleep anyway, so I came over."

A sharp crackling from the vicinity of the workbench caused us both to jump. Weston had turned on the electric arc that vapourized part of the bead. He slid a panel in place over the exposed film and came to join us. It was clear from his first words that he had been listening.

"So you've some new information. Please feel free to confide in us." Geoffrey took a seat and waited for a response.

"Well," Heath began, "about two weeks ago my son and I went to a Rugby match. I'm afraid I left my keys in the car. When we came out of the stadium, they were still there. But I noticed traces of clay on some of them. Peter thought I had probably dropped my chain on the ground sometime earlier, but now I wonder."

"And Peter is your son?" Weston asked.

"Yes."

"How many keys had *no* clay on them?"

"Let me see. I believe the house keys were clean. And there was the key to the motorcar . . ."

"In other words," Geoffrey prompted, "the only keys which may have had impressions made from them were those to the laboratory?"

"Yes, I believe so. There's a safe deposit key on the chain, too. But I don't remember seeing anything on it."

"Have you washed them since then?"

"I've wiped them off," the doctor confessed.

"Ah, then let me have a look."

Heath fished the chain from his pocket and handed it to my partner. Geoffrey took out his glass and closely inspected each key—as well as the chain itself.

"Just as I had hoped," he commented. "If you look very closely, you will see a small speck that has eluded your polishing. It's right there in the center of the 'A' in the manufacturer's name. It appears to be modeling clay—something one would hardly find in a mud puddle. Observe also that there is absolutely nothing lodged in the crevices in the chain. Your keys did not take a tumble. They were deliberately duplicated."

As he finished speaking, Weston got up and began banging drawers in search of a needle. Finding one, he used it to remove the bit of evidence from the "A." He then placed the clay in an envelope; sealed, dated, and initialed the container; and had Dr. Heath write his own name and the source of the clay on the back flap. That done, Geoffrey sat down and resumed questioning.

"Doesn't it strike you as odd, Doctor, that only the Pinehurst Laboratory keys were copied?"

"Not at all," our visitor replied. "My own keys are very common ones. The car key even has the name of the motorcar company written on it."

"The one to the safe deposit box would also be obvious," Geoffrey agreed. "But the front door key—the one to your house—is an entirely different matter. Who would know its use? I'm afraid that whoever made those impressions was well acquainted with either the laboratory keys or with those to your house."

"Impossible!"

"Why so?" Weston inquired.

"Because I know my workers! The guards already have keys. So do some of the scientists and technicians. And I can vouch for anyone who doesn't."

"And can you," Geoffrey prodded, "vouch for your family and friends as well?"

"Now you have gone too far," Heath responded

icily. "I won't sit here and listen to you accusing my wife and child."

"Heath, I'm not accusing anyone. But I am suspecting everyone. That's my job. As a matter of fact, if I were accusing anyone, it would most likely be you. You are the only man, so far, who can be demonstrated to have had an opportunity to steal the papers. You had the combination to the safe. You could have removed the papers at *any* time in the past and replaced them with an empty folder. It would have been an easy matter then to have staged discovery of the crime last night. It all fits together. And if the papers have a ready buyer, we have our motive."

Heath seemed genuinely startled. The wildness of the hunted flickered for an instant across his features. The conversation was not taking at all the turn that he had expected.

"Then why don't you call the Inspector," he asked, "and have me arrested?"

Weston eyed him steadily.

"You can thank God for two things—a dead dog and a glass bead. I, frankly, don't believe you're guilty."

"I do not thank fairy tale creatures," the scientist stated stiffly. "But I do appreciate your seeing some benefit for me in the dog and the bead."

"May I ask you, Doctor, why you don't believe in God?"

Arthur Heath seemed relieved at the change of subject. He relaxed a bit. Hands together with finger tips touching, he looked almost as though he were some professor back at the university.

"It is quite simple," he assured us. "I admire the reasoning in Anthony Flew's parable about the gardener. Two explorers come across a clearing in the forest filled with flowers and weeds. One man supposes that a gardener tends the plot. They wait to see him, but nobody comes. The man declares that the gardener is invisible. So they put out barbed wire and dogs. But they find no gardener. The believer concludes that there is an invisible, undetectable gardener. But his friend argues that there is no difference between that kind of gardener and none at all.

"There are a lot of flowers and a tremendous number of weeds in this world, Weston. And I see no gardener. I don't see one because none exists. Man is the measure of all things—man, who has pulled himself up from the ooze and is aiming for the stars."

Geoffrey's eyes never wavered from our guest.

"Heath," he declared, "you amaze me. You reject an invisible gardener but are only too happy to accept the idea of an invisible thief if it will save your skin."

"The situations aren't the same at all!" the scientist disagreed. "The thief takes papers. The gardener does nothing."

"Nothing?" Weston asked. "The flowers grow. The weeds grow. And who are you to say that the weeds are worthless or even that they are weeds? Perhaps the gardener gives the plants freedom to compete. Who is responsible for the rain? When I study crime, I see cause and effect—with human decision-making as the root. When I study nature, I see cause and effect, symmetry, beauty, and the prima-facie evidence of a planner. All you see is beneficent ooze.

"If God created man, is it so odd that He can avoid human detection? And who can blame God for not subjecting himself to man's idle curiosity? I am convinced, though, that He does not always limit himself to working behind the scenes. Witnesses throughout history—people with no vested interest—have testified to quite remarkable interventions. Over a hundred, for example,

declared that they saw Jesus Christ after He arose
physically from the grave. Their accounts agreed. They
held to their story in the face of torture and sang while
being murdered. Even such pagan and Jewish enemies as
Suetonius, Thallus, and Josephus admitted as much.
What possible motive, Doctor, would drive men and
women to die for what they knew to be a lie? And if they
died for the truth, then God entered history as a man.
There's your gardener."

"I wish I could believe that," Heath replied. There
was a touch of sadness in his voice. "But I've lived too
long and seen too much. My father, Weston, died in the
mines. He was the best-natured, most honest man I ever
knew. I saw his twisted body as they brought it out! A
good God would have prevented that accident!

"I've clawed my way to where I am now. In college I
was never brilliant. I made up for it with extra hours of
study. And, frankly, I have no use for a god anymore. I
believe in hard work.

"Weston, I have textbooks in my library that are
only twenty years old but full of errors. Last year's fact
is this year's joke. Truth develops. And as far as I'm
concerned, Jesus and the Bible are for some bygone era
when people were more superstitious and needed
religion. Evolution may be brutal, but then so is life. I
put my confidence in man—in what he is and what he
will become."

Weston poured some tea from the pitcher. He
looked down into his cup for a second—as though
searching for the right words.

"Arthur, I have experienced tragedy in my life, too.
So I know what you went through. But I believe you're
wrong in your conclusions—dangerously wrong. Believing as you do, what possible meaning can you see in
your life?"

"I live," Heath declared, "for my work. Our experiments at Pinehurst could make the world a better place."

Weston gazed with new understanding at the doctor's tired features.

"So that's why the theft has hit you so hard! If research stops, you become a failure. Your outlook on life is certainly a hard taskmaster."

"And how would you feel," the scientist replied, "if something that you'd been working on for years collapsed? You surely wouldn't turn handsprings."

"No," Geoffrey admitted. "But neither would I feel that my life had lost its meaning. God declares that I have intrinsic worth. I believe Him."

"You're a fortunate man, Weston, to be able to accept that. But I can't. There is no room in my system for the supernatural."

"So much for your objectivity," my partner lamented.

"Honestly," Heath countered, "I'm surprised that a man of your stature could be so childlike. I envy your simplicity, but I look down on it all the same."

"What is honesty?" Geoffrey replied. "And of what stature am I? If your system is correct, no one has stature. Man is a mere animal—the product of slime. He is of no more value than his source. He lives. He dies. So what? The wise man dies like the fool, and nothing has meaning."

"And yet," Heath suggested, "civilization progresses."

Weston looked pained.

"Show me that it progresses in any manner other than materialistically. The civilization you picture is nothing but a collection of dying men trying to climb onto the shoulders of the dead so that their own clavicles

can in turn be mounted by the, as yet, unborn. What is
society? Some have equated it with the state and served
the whim of tyrants. Others have pictured it as the entire
human race. But mankind has so many conflicting and
mutually exclusive goals! Even when you decide what
civilization is, what gives *it* meaning? Surely it is worth
no more than the sum of its parts. If man is worthless, so
is society. And society is anything but eternal. Einstein
saw what his bomb could do and said something to the
effect of, 'After all, it's only a very tiny planet.' He knew
how near our own extinction might be. If somebody
presses that button, then where is your civilization *and*
your life's work? Down the drain!"

Geoffrey's last remark evidently hit home. Heath's
cheeks flushed and his voice faltered ever so slightly.

"Weston, I cannot believe that that will ever happen.
Man has established law by social compact and is learning to govern himself in an orderly manner. I *will not*
believe that all of his achievements will be destroyed."

"Your faith in man is commendable," my partner
noted with irony. "But what facts do you base it on?
You mistakenly reject God because of a personal mis-
fortune. What will it take to get you to reject man? That
social compact law you mentioned filled Nazi gas cham-
bers, built slave labor camps in Siberia, carried out the
Inquisition, aborted millions of unborn babies, drove
the Indians from their lands, and I could go on and on.
Is that the mankind you are so optimistic about? You
make man the creator of law. Can you stomach those
laws that he has used to liquidate his neighbors? If there
is no law above the law—if there is no God—then all
law is relative. If, as you say, truth is developing, then
there is no real right or wrong. Law becomes a fraud.
And what is there really to stay the finger on the button?"

Arthur Heath's fingers drummed incessantly on the arm of the chair. He was thinking rapidly—realizing that he had been put at a disadvantage.

"Law makes ordered living possible," he asserted. "Even bad laws are better than none at all. And although law *is* relative, it can be effective in limiting violence."

"But don't you see," Geoffrey replied, "that law only works when people consider it to be grounded in an absolute—sometimes not even then. Without citizens that have convictions concerning right and wrong, society would crumble. And your own definition of law makes law (if you will allow the use of the term) evil."

"You're twisting my words," the doctor protested. "I never said law was either good or evil. It is simply useful in bringing about desired results."

" 'Desired results?' What does that mean?"

"Why," Heath answered, "that law produces the greatest good for the greatest number."

"What is 'good'?"

"Why, what benefits the citizens."

"How," Weston shot back, "do you define 'benefit'?"

"As whatever causes the greatest social ah . . ."

"You see, Heath," Geoffrey continued helpfully, "it all boils down to some value judgments. And that is precisely what your system can neither contain nor tolerate. Once man is an animal and nothing more (or the programmed machine that Skinner has suggested), what right have you to speak of 'good' or 'benefit'? Remove God from your view of the universe, and *every* moral interpretation goes out the window as well. You can't even hold that *life* is 'good.' As a matter of fact, if survival of the fittest produced man and if man is still on the way 'up,' then anything (such as law) which reduces competition results in the slowing of that 'upward' movement. Society and law protect the weak—allowing the unfit to survive. Law and society must therefore be rejected. Murder becomes the greatest 'good.' Mass executions are transformed into events to be celebrated. Cunning and theft turn laudable. But to be blunt about it, you are a traitor to your own philosophy! You squealed like a stuck pig when your papers were stolen. You really should have jumped up and down and shouted, 'good show!' But you can't live within your own system. Deep down inside, you know it's flawed. You still believe that there are absolutes—that theft and murder, for instance, are wrong. You *know* that there's a difference between the death of a dog and the death of a man. You realize subconsciously that God made you in His image. It's your rebellion against Him that prevents you from seeing what you know."

"Mr. Weston," the doctor replied with a tinge of boredom, "you argue well from the point of view of your system. I'm suitably impressed. But if I ended up rejecting man, I still doubt that I'd accept the existence of a god. It would seem more manly to me to simply accept life as being purposeless. The conversation has been most interesting. But I'm rather tired. And I did come here, after all, to discuss the investigation—not to become embroiled in religious speculation."

"Indeed you did," my partner agreed. "But I would hardly say that we have been digressing. In my investigations I do not merely study events and physical evidence. People, after all, commit crimes. I observe people. These last few moments, I have been having a look at you."

"And what did you see?" Heath responded—now fully alert.

"I saw a man whose ethics are no more than relative. I saw a scientist engaged in research about which I am more and more curious. And I wondered about two things. What was the real motive of our thief? And how much of what you told me about the keys was the truth? Your whole concept of truth is, after all, inadequate."

"You yourself have noted," Arthur Heath reminded him, "that my relativism is more theoretical than practical. I assure you that you can accept everything that I have said about the keys as being factual. And I congratulate you on your technique. You certainly are adept at pulling information out of a man. I don't believe you ever say anything without having a reason."

"I try to know where I'm going," Geoffrey acknowledged.

"I'm sure you do. Just see to it that you remember that I'm innocent. The bead and the dog and all that!" With those words our visitor stood up to signal his intention to leave.

"Thank you very much for spending a few moments with us," I told him. "I've enjoyed listening to you two tearing into each other."

"And," Weston invited, "if you should recall anything else, we certainly would like to hear from you."

Arthur Heath gave no indication that he had heard that last remark. I doubted that he would volunteer anything in the future. Weston and the doctor walked together to the door. My partner opened it a crack and then turned toward our guest.

"One last question before you go. Who, besides you, knows the combination to the safe?"

Heath smiled sardonically. "I'm the only one, Weston. The only one."

So saying, he strode through the door and out into the night. Geoffrey stood looking after him for a moment and then, with an exuberant briskness, retraced his steps through the living room.

"John, what a case this is!" he fairly exploded. "It has everything—technical problems, secret papers, and a lying witness!"

"You don't think he was telling the truth then about the keys?"

"Oh, I'm sure he wasn't," Geoffrey replied. "Keys to secret laboratories simply are not left in open motorcars at Rugby matches. And if they were, the thief would make impressions of all the keys—not of only the necessary ones. Someone other than the good doctor may have played with the modeling clay; but, if so, Heath has an idea of who that person is. The man is clearly shielding somebody. And it's not impossible that the whole business about the keys might have been staged by Heath himself. The clay on them looked just a little too clean to have been collecting dirt in a pocket for two weeks."

"I presume then," I concluded, "that we concentrate on the doctor's friends and family."

"Oh, absolutely," Weston agreed. "Some talks with neighbors and with acquaintances will no doubt prove helpful. And I hope Twigg's profiles on the employees will shed a little light. John, will you take over developing the spectrograph? I have some thinking to do."

"Why I'd be delighted to," I propositioned, "if you'll answer one question for me. Why didn't Heath dismiss you? He didn't even seem particularly angry when you doubted his truthfulness."

Geoffrey smiled somewhat ruefully.

"I don't imagine," he observed, "that our employer is quite righteous enough for righteous indignation. And to fire me would only cast suspicion upon himself. He had to settle for my conviction that he himself did not steal the papers."

True to my word, I trudged to the darkroom carrying the photographic plate. Geoffrey lay back in the recliner and closed his eyes—to think. That's the last I saw of him for the next few moments. When I emerged, he was watching television. It was, however, the most boring program in the history of the media. I couldn't resist a comment or two.

"Well, well, I see they've finally cleaned up the tele. Suggestive humour, violence, and bad acting are all gone! Don't you think they could have kept the actors, though? I saw a Japanese movie once in which no one spoke. All that the characters did was to carry water up a mountain and pour it on their crops. But at least it had somewhat of a rhythm to it—up and down, up and down. That thing you're watching has nothing."

"Isn't it interesting, though," Weston concurred. "Twigg's messenger brought it over about ten minutes ago—along with that envelope over there."

My companion waved his hand toward a thick pouch on the dining room table. It obviously contained extracts of Pinehurst's personnel files—along with anything additional that the Yard had dug up. I pulled up a chair and settled down to watch two hours of uninterrupted Pinehurst Laboratory corridor. Weston advised me on how to get the most out of the production.

"Keep your eyes on that infrared receiver. If it disappears, let me know."

The receiver, however, did not disappear. As I continued concentrating on that one spot, I began to feel like a driver too long at the wheel. Weston's exclamation jolted me upright.

"There it is! That's it. By George, we're on the trail!"

"What is it?" I wanted to know. "Can't you let a

chap sleep in peace? I don't see anything."

Geoffrey stepped over to the reel-to-reel unit and backed up the tape. He then let it advance at normal speed for a few seconds and stopped the image. Kneeling in front of the television, he pointed out a tiny, dark spot just in view on the screen. It seemed to have emerged from the shadows at about a height of five feet.

"I'll start the tape again," he continued. "Watch what happens."

He pushed a button. The spot resumed its advance along the corridor for a few feet—then disappeared. Geoffrey stopped the action again.

"You'll notice now," he observed, "that an identical spot has appeared about two feet in front of the one that vanished."

His finger came down on the button a second time. The dot continued its advance toward the laboratory. It, in turn, also vanished—to be replaced by another farther along. The sequence repeated itself until the last spot left camera range.

"What is it?" I inquired. "Are you sure it's not just a defect in the film?"

"Not on your life." Weston slowly shook his head. "That is our thief! It's the cleverest scheme I've ever seen. We're dealing with a genius. I don't know what Heath has in his laboratory, but it must be absolutely unique to inspire this performance. Let's play the second act and find out the time of the crime."

Geoffrey rewound the tape and replaced it with a second reel from the top of the console. The new tape spun forward at high speed until roughly the same amount of tape was on the take-up reel that had been there during act one when the dots appeared. From that point we began viewing at normal speed. Within five minutes the mysterious specks danced onto the screen and hopscotched to the safe. The clock on the wall showed twelve thirty-two. Weston stopped the action.

"Get some pictures of that, John. We'll need one taken of a dot just before it vanishes. Blow the print up just as much as screen resolution will allow. And I'd also like a series of shots to show progression."

As I began taking pictures, he retrieved the spectrograph that I had hung up to dry in the darkroom. Soon he was pouring over volumes of sample readings that he had worked up as a reference file. I interrupted his concentration.

"Geoffrey, you'll be making comparisons for several hours. And I don't know how you do it. I'm so tired already that my vision is blurring. It's getting light outside, and I've got the dots on film. I'm going to bed. The developing can wait. I'd advise you to close your eyes for a while, too."

Without waiting for an answer, I headed for my room.

CHAPTER 4

Murder by Philosophy

The faint crackle of bacon cooking on the skillet brought me back to life at about nine-thirty that morning. I quickly dressed and followed my nose to the kitchen. Passing Weston's bedroom on the way, I saw that he had not so much as rumpled the bedspread. If he had slept, it had been on the recliner.

When I reached my destination, I found my friend—head still damp from a shower—busily cracking eggs and toasting muffins. The bacon was already on the table.

"Well, it's about time," Geoffrey chided. He glanced in my direction. "Do you realize that you've slept three entire hours? There's work to do. The game's afoot. I can smell adventure in the air!"

I disagreed.

"You're just giddy from a lack of sleep."

"Well," he rejoined, "at least you'll admit there's bacon in the air."

"Which is all the adventure I want until after breakfast. And I'll take coffee instead of the usual tea."

I found a couple of plates and set the table. Geoffrey brought the pan over and scooped out the contents. It was not Hugh Boone egg scramble. But it *was* eggs. I put some coffee in the cups and poured. After giving thanks that the Lord had thus far protected me from my partner's cooking, we began eating. The food was not fancy, but it had an honest, wholesome flavor.

My curiosity got the better of me.

"What," I asked, "did you find out while I was asleep?"

"I found out," he answered with a smile, "that one can hear you snoring from all the way in the living room."

"Oh bother!" I breathed. "At times you can be the most exasperating person on earth. What of the experiments, man? What have you discovered?"

Weston's smile faded. He was now all business.

"I haven't been able to get exact percentages of the elements and compounds in the glass. I can tell you, though, that those black wafers are carbon. The glass itself seems fairly normal—though of high quality. I've listed the ingredients along the edge of the spectograph."

"And the prints of the pictures I took?"

"You'll find them," Geoffrey answered, "in the living room."

My mind won out over my stomach. I left the table and returned in a moment with a stack of eight-by-ten glossies. Sitting down once again, I began sipping coffee and studying the prints. From time to time Weston pointed out unusual features.

"Look at the picture taken of the dot as it was disappearing," he advised. "You will notice that the spot seems to close in from the two sides. And it forms a very slight crescent just before vanishing. Observe also that the series pictures show a constant distance between the point at which one dot disappears and at which the next one jumps into view. Furthermore, the enlargement reveals a slight sparkle in the center of the spot. I take it to be light reflected from glass."

"What do you make of it all?" I inquired.

"Oh, I know what it is," my partner replied, "But I don't enjoy being laughed at. When my plans are finished and I can duplicate the effect, I'll tell you *and* the Inspector."

"In other words," I complained, "you're going to be secretive."

"I'm afraid so."

"Geoffrey," I declared with conviction, "you're impossible! You really should have taken up a career in the theatre. Your flair for the dramatic is beyond bounds! You—"

I was interrupted in mid sentence by the jangling of the telephone. My friend saw his opportunity to escape an argument, and he took it. As his back disappeared into the living room, I found myself without an audience. Realizing that Weston's conversations on the telephone were, as often as not, followed by prolonged action, I set about eating in earnest. I was just cleaning the last crumb from my plate when Geoffrey returned. At first sight of him I knew that something was wrong— very wrong. The color had drained from his face. Waxen numbness and unbelieving horror mingled in his eyes.

"I've killed him, John," he declared matter of factly. "I've killed him."

"Killed whom?" I asked. "What has happened?"

Weston sat down and sipped his coffee in silence. Then he spoke slowly—almost mechanically.

"At six-fifteen this morning a shot was fired at Heath's house in Reigate. As nearly as anyone can determine, Dr. Arthur Heath blew his brains out. His wife found a note by the body. It read: 'Man's future is not what I thought it would be. Humanity is worthless. So why continue the game?' It had to be my arguments that drove him to the edge."

I paused and let the news penetrate. Two or three of Geoffrey's remarks to Heath came to mind. And I could see how my colleague felt.

"How horrible!" I sympathized. "But surely it was his own philosophy that killed him—not your words."

"His philosophy, yes," my partner conceded. "But my words played a part. I dare say he would be alive today if I had not said what I said. I caused his philosophy to crumble, and he crumbled with it. He had invested too much of his life into serving a lie. In the end, he could not abandon his convictions. He chose to abandon living."

"But," I pointed out, "he seemed anything but despondent when he left last night. I cannot believe that he was a man preparing for suicide."

Weston's fist hit the table with a loud bang.

"You're right, John. You're right. Something else must have happened—something which reinforced what I said. But what? We've a trip ahead of us to Reigate! Grab the personnel file. You can read it to me on the way."

Within three minutes we were speeding down Baker Street. Tires squealed as we made the turns. Once again we headed for the southwest.

During the trip I alternated between holding on for my life and reading. Of the twenty-three scientists and technicians employed by Pinehurst Laboratory, four proved to be of special interest to Geoffrey. Albert Post had once been employed by the Germans. Niles Gilbert was a devotee of yoga. Mary Starling had worked for an optician before she came to Pinehurst. And James Smyth had an I.Q. that tested near two hundred. The other workers would have to be investigated as well, but we would begin with these.

Weston pulled the car over to the curb a little up the street from an old brownstone. Police cars all but blocked the roadway in front of the house. And a couple of bobbies stood outside, keeping curious neighbors at a distance. Without hesitation, we walked up to one of the policemen and identified ourselves. We were allowed to pass.

As we climbed the steps, we could hear voices emanating from the room to our right. Just inside, we turned in that direction and came upon a large living room that fronted on the street. Twigg, Inspector Cyril Manchester, and three others were busily at work. Manchester was minutely examining ashes in the fireplace. Another—a Mr. Dutworth, I believe—was lifting prints. And two gentlemen were photographing the room from every angle. Rather surprisingly, the corpse was still in residence. Twigg, who had just finished writing an entry into his notebook, came over to greet us.

"I see you two are late again, as usual." He extended his hand to both of us. "I decided to keep the body here so you could have a firsthand look at it. He appears almost alive slumped over there on the armchair, doesn't he. One might surmise that he wanted to gaze out that window just one last time as he pulled the trigger."

"Or," Weston interrupted, "that someone wanted us to think that."

"Obviously," Twigg agreed. "We do not generally investigate suicides so thoroughly."

"You have some evidence then," I prompted, "that—"

"Only Mrs. Heath's claim that she heard voices

arguing downstairs sometime before the shot."

"At what time?" Geoffrey asked.

"Your guess is as good as mine," the Inspector responded. "She says she was half asleep and didn't look at the clock. We don't know by how long the voices preceded the man's death."

"Have you," I inquired, "formed any theory?"

Twigg folded his arms and stared at us before answering. He was almost daring us to disagree.

"John, I think Heath stole the papers. Someone threatened to expose him. Rather than spend the rest of his life in gaol, he stuck a pistol barrel into his mouth and pulled the trigger."

"Then why," Geoffrey objected, "was there no confession in the note?"

"He was a proud man, Weston. He may not have wanted the disgrace."

"And suicide is no disgrace?" my partner asked with a touch of sarcasm. "Come now!"

"He was under stress," Twigg reasoned. "Who of us is completely logical when we are upset?"

"Who, indeed? But," Geoffrey suggested, "isn't it possible that Heath suspected someone else of the robbery? He then confronted the thief and was killed for his trouble."

"And the note?"

"Ah, the note. I presume you have determined that it is not a forgery."

"It is genuine." The Inspector smiled as he made the pronouncement.

"And you deduce that—if forced to write the note—Heath would have confessed to the crime. The real thief would then have no worries this side of Judgment."

"Absolutely," Twigg agreed.

"But," Geoffrey challenged, "what if it was not a

suicide note at all that you found? What if the man had simply written a personal memorandum about something that was bothering him. All that the note says is: 'Man's future is not what I thought it would be. Humanity is worthless. So why continue the game?' Does he mean 'Why should I continue the game of living?' Or is he saying 'Why should mankind continue the game of life?' If he meant the latter, then our real thief could have simply taken the note off the desk or table and set it by the body. As a matter of fact, Heath paid us a visit at Baker Street last night. And I told him that man might blow himself up."

"You didn't!"

"I'm afraid I did, Twigg. But, as Taylor will tell you, the doctor did not seem to take what I said especially seriously."

"Well," the Inspector remarked, "it seems we now have two theories—your speculation and mine. Let's have some proof one way or the other. I know how much you enjoy my absence while you conduct your investigations. So I think I'll get on with some work elsewhere. I trust you won't be too inconvenienced by the other officers. Happy hunting." He put on his hat and left the room.

We lost no time in getting to work ourselves. I began an inch-by-inch search of the rug. Weston went directly to the body. He took out his ever-present lens and examined the dead man's lips. Then he scrutinized nose, forehead and neck. That done, he busied himself pulling Heath's hair aside and inspecting the scalp, bit by bit. He reminded me of a barber in search of dandruff or of a doctor looking for ticks.

Geoffrey's attention now turned to the body's hands. Removing a nail file from my bag, he made scrapings from under each of the victim's fingernails. He placed the smears in an envelope. Then, after examining both arms under the lens, he took a scraping from the left forearm.

Meanwhile, my own investigation was bearing fruit. I found a generous supply of what looked like dog hair clinging to the fibers of the carpet. But of more interest, I also uncovered some long blond strands that were undoubtedly human hair, some grey ones which seemed to match the pate of the dead man, AND A SINGLE GLASS BEAD!"

"Look here, will you!" I cried to Weston. "It appears that Twigg may be right, after all!"

My friend came over and held the bead up under his glass.

"This is certainly interesting," he murmured. "As you have no doubt surmised, it is identical with the one we stumbled across at the laboratory. But why do you feel its presence here supports Twigg's view of the case?"

"Why because Heath must have had a supply of the beads. That makes him our prime suspect, does it not?"

"But," Weston disagreed, "he had no need of them. Heath could enter and leave the laboratory at will. Why would he go to the bother of creating an illusion? No, the bead cannot tie the doctor in with the crime. But it certainly connects him with the thief. Our employer was murdered for what he knew."

"It is murder, then."

"Of a sort, Taylor. Of a sort. But I've never seen anything quite like it. It may be a case of cold, calculated murder by words."

"Blackmail! Oh, the poor devil," I sympathized. "What kind of monster would force a man to kill himself by threatening to expose some indiscretion unless he blew his own brains out?"

"What kind of monster, indeed!" Geoffrey nodded

his head in agreement. "Or perhaps some subtle and even more diabolical form of persuasion was used. Remember that our murderer is extremely clever. The person who outwitted Pinehurst's security system is capable of almost anything. Here, let me help you finish searching the rug."

For nearly an hour the two of us were on our hands and knees—picking at warp and woof. The effort yielded a collection of hairs, some cigarette ash, and a trace of mud. At last satisfied that we would find no more, Weston asked one of the detectives where we might find the dead man's widow and his son. Following directions, we arrived at the back porch. Susanna Heath was seated there on a lawn chair. She was staring into the backyard—a statue oblivious to everything but the pain of the morning. What must have been her son— a lad of about seventeen—was standing on a ladder pruning a tree. Geoffrey's voice was gentle as he addressed the woman.

"Mrs. Heath, I know how difficult it is for you to speak now. But I have some questions that I must ask. Your husband wanted me to investigate the matter at Pinehurst. I think he would want me to look into the circumstances of his death, as well."

"You're very kind." For a fleeting second her mouth managed a half smile. "I'll help if I can."

"Did your husband seem at all worried prior to the robbery?"

"Not at all," she replied. "He was happy. There were no financial problems. He enjoyed his work and was kept busy."

"Has he had any visitors during the last few days?"

"Only Niles and Mary."

"That would be Niles Gilbert?" Geoffrey prompted.

"Yes, and Mary Starling. The two are dating. And

Niles lives just three houses down from here. He has been a friend of Arthur's for years."

"Did your husband," Weston asked, "have a hobby room or laboratory here at home?"

"Why yes. Would you like to see it?"

"We certainly would," I declared.

Mrs. Heath escorted us inside once more. She stopped at the door leading to the cellar stairs.

"It's down there." Her voice quivered ever so slightly. "That part of the house is filled with memories. Do you mind going on alone?"

"Not at all," my partner assured her. "We may have some further questions, but I don't imagine we'll have any difficulty finding you after we take a look around."

"I'll be on the porch if you need me," she promised.

Mrs. Susanna Heath turned and walked in the direction of the backyard. I found the light switch, and Geoffrey and I began our descent. Fifty-year-old boards creaked under our feet. The room at the end of the stairway, however, proved to be thoroughly modern. Arthur Heath, it turns out, was one of those fellows who had almost as many gadgets at home as he had at the office. The place was filled with such items as test tubes, Petri dishes, saws, mechanic's tools, and electronics testing equipment. One entire wall was lined with shelf upon shelf of scientific texts. An electron microscope in the corner must have cost the man a not-so-small fortune. I let out a low whistle.

"Weston, Heath had to have been a blooming obsessive-compulsive! I've never seen such a collection of tools under one roof. There are at least four complete shops here. And the whole thing looks like some sort of display. Even the flasks are lined up like tin soldiers!"

"Things do seem rather more ordered down here than in the living quarters," my companion observed dryly. "If you find a bottle marked 'CLUE,' let me know." He walked over to the books and started to browse. A volume caught his eye, and he began skimming its pages.

"Fortunately, John, our late employer was in the habit of underlining what interested him. I think I shall find this reading most illuminating." Weston became absorbed in his studies.

Workbenches lined all but one wall of the room. I set about pulling out drawers and opening doors. On the bottom shelf of the cabinet that was under the electronics bench, I found a two-gallon pickle jar.

"Weston," I chuckled, "you told me to let you know."

"To know what?"

"Not what," I corrected, "when. I've discovered the bottle marked 'CLUE.' "

"You're joking!" His face showed understandable surprise.

"Well, that's not the exact word on the label," I conceded. "But I don't think you'll quibble." I held up the jar so that he could see the bold letters printed across its front: 'OPTICAL BEADS.' Only an inch or so of the beads remained in the bottom.

Geoffrey stepped over, picked out a pinch, and examined the grains under his glass. His nod was one of satisfaction.

"There's virtue in order after all," he observed. "How large a surface area could one cover with the seven quarts or so that we may assume are missing?"

"I imagine quite a few square yards. But the jar may not have been full."

"No," he agreed, "it may not have been. But I don't believe it was far from it. The doctor strikes me as the kind of man who would match the size of the pile to the size of the container. Besides, it would take at least that amount in order to construct the machine used in entering Pinehurst."

"But by saying that," I pointed out, "you've convicted the man. What possible use could he have for two quarts of beads other than for burglarizing the laboratory?"

"I think the answer to that, old fellow, is right under our noses." Geoffrey reached over to a large white box on the workbench and flipped a switch on its side. The front of the box was evidently a projection screen, for it flashed to life—becoming a vivid mountain scene. An old truck was struggling up a winding road toward the point from which the motion picture was taken. As I moved my head up, down, or to the sides, I was startled to see that the angle of view of the picture likewise changed. I could see different scenery at the edges.

"Weston, this is remarkable! The box is like a window."

"It is indeed," he responded. "I believe Heath was working on the ultimate in three-dimensional cinema. He may have even envisioned adapting the process to television. You'll have to agree that a two-quart supply is hardly excessive in view of such goals. Unfortunately, someone else saw an entirely different application for Heath's box. We have here stage one of the device our thief used."

"How so?"

"If you examine this screen, you will find that it is covered with thousands of those mysterious beads. On the inside are several projectors which no doubt employ mirrors to present their images to the screen at various angles. Each film was shot from different positions. Each projected image covers the entire screen. But the beads are selective in what they will pass. Each one that is tilted toward a given light source projects only the light from that source. The result is that, although several images appear on the same screen, only one or two can be seen at a time. As the viewer moves around, he sees different images. The illusion is created that he is watching the same scene from a changing perspective."

"But how," I objected, "does that get a thief anywhere?"

"It doesn't in itself," Weston admitted. "But think about the principle. Extend one of those crescent-shaped scuffs on the Pinehurst floor into a full circle. Erect a cone over the circle—better yet, build the thing in the form of a bullet. Make it of clear plastic. Glue on several hundred thousand beads at appropriate degrees of tilt. Leave some tiny clear spots in the plastic, and mount either light canals leading to television cameras or the miniature cameras themselves to those spots. Cut a door in the side of your bullet. Place a yoke inside the machine and wire around the yoke to projectors directly opposite each camera. Now what do you have? You have a device that projects light from whatever direction onto a screen on its opposite side. A man in the yoke becomes invisible. So many images are projected on any given portion of screen that an outsider might be looking at an edge of it at exactly a ninety degree angle to another man looking at the same portion. One person sees the scenery behind the machine as viewed from his position. The other sees entirely different scenery—what he would see from his angle if the bullet were not there. Here, let me draw you a sketch."

Weston took a note pad from his pocket and scrawled a diagram. But I was unconvinced. And I told him so.

"Geoffrey, I don't think it will work. What about keystoning? You can't project a flat image onto a curved surface without causing distortion."

"No," he agreed, "but you can use a lens system on the cameras to induce pre-distortion. The curved viewing screen then corrects for the deformity in what is being projected. Or you can employ a computer similar to the one that unscrambled signals from the Jupiter lander or which reconstructed the voice of Enrico Caruso from wax cylinders. Such a computer would offer a double advantage. It would not only correct for distortion, but could also fill in any gaps in the same way that our brain fills in the two blind spots before our eyes. So equipped, the machine could fill in the earth under it so that it would not be detectable from above. The same system might also lock a scene in its memory and continue projecting it even after the cameras on the other side were shut off. It would allow our thief, in other words, to hide behind the bullet and open the safe while the guards saw nothing. The man could remove the papers, climb back into the bullet through its door, reset the computer to live action, and go merrily on his way without anyone being the wiser."

"Good heavens!" I replied in a stunned half-whisper. "What you're talking about is the most important military invention since the hydrogen bomb!"

"Precisely. And that's what makes me so curious about the researches at Pinehurst Laboratory. If an invention of such magnitude was risked in order to obtain the papers, then what kind of doomsday machine is being developed in there?"

"But," I asked, "was there really very much of a risk?"

"Oh, certainly. Those dark spots on the viewer in the guard's office were the lens openings for the cameras. Each was seen for only a certain number of degrees and then disappeared. The crescent shape of the spot as it vanished was caused by the curvature of the bullet. Now normally these would not be noticed. The human mind would ignore them in much the same way that it ignores its own optical blind spots. But there was just a chance that one of the guards might have reacted.

"Yet none did," I pointed out.

"You're wrong. Tom Yancy saw them clearly—in his subconscious. They made him uneasy. But he never quite knew why."

"Surely, though, there was little chance of being detected."

"But there was a chance." As he talked, Geoffrey began snapping pictures of the white box. "There was also a possibility that the cameras would not project a high enough intensity of infrared to keep the alarm from sounding. Notice how the interloper scraped against the wall to increase his chances. Of course he might also have had an infrared light source inside the bullet."

"How did he see?"

"Through a television screen inside the machine."

"And how," I asked, "was all this powered?"

"Now there you have another risk factor." Geoffrey pocketed his camera. "The bullet must contain a large number of fuel cells. Obviously the weight of electronics and batteries made the thing extremely cumbersome. Consider the scuffs on the floor. And I doubt that there was electricity enough to power it for more than an hour."

"Then the thief must have been athletic," I summarized. "It was probably a man. And he had to count upon getting into and out of the installation rather quickly."

"Yes, and there was always the danger that he might be seen by the guards at the perimeter."

"How so?"

"Through his shadow," Weston explained. "If he crossed the beam of a searchlight, he could not project that light onto the ground in front of him. Furthermore, the only way that he could enter and leave the grounds was through the front gate. There was no other way to get such a heavy machine past the fence."

"So how did he escape?"

"You will remember that the crime took place at precisely 12:32—although the thief must have gained entrance at some time prior to that. Arthur Heath drove up to the gate at 1:45. Our friend saw the automobile lights in the distance and came to the gate while the guards were concentrating on the new arrival. When the gates were opened to admit Heath, our 'invisible man' (or perhaps our 'invisible woman') simply walked through the gate. He or she must have gotten in in much the same way. The outside guards change their posts at midnight—opening the gate in the process."

"Then," I pointed out, "you have to be wrong about the amount of time that the machine can operate. You're already talking about an hour and forty-five minutes—with no guarantee that an automobile is going to drive up."

"Possibly the system is more efficient than I suppose, or the fuel cells stronger. But it also may be that the thief hid in the doorway to one of the buildings and only activated the bullet when he heard a guard approaching. In that way he could probably hold out until the gates were opened for employees in the morning. The guard on patrol is, of course, an additional risk."

"But that brings us back to your first question," I complained. "What could be going on in the laboratories that would cause our thief to risk such a machine?"

"Exactly, John. This case is far from over. We know

the how, but we haven't a clue as to the why or the who. And we still lack the how concerning poor Heath's murder. I'm not prepared to accept your blackmail idea. If blackmail were the order of the day, it would most likely be the blackmailer with the bullet in his brain. Heath would be busily explaining away the evidence."

"Yet I take it," I guessed, "that there was no blow to Heath's head."

"I could find neither bruises nor contusions," Weston admitted.

"His lips show none of the tiny burns which one would expect if chloroform were forced upon him. Of course he might have eaten something and collapsed. But I have my doubts. One does not accuse someone of a crime and then accept cookies from him. It does not appear that there is any skin under the doctor's nails as evidence of a struggle. We'll have to put some smears under the microscope to be sure of that. His knuckles are not bruised. I could detect no needle marks—though a needle could have been stuck through his clothes. In all, unless the medical examiner comes up with some unusual chemical inside the body—which I doubt—Dr. Heath shot himself."

"There were powder traces on his hand?"

"Yes," Geoffrey responded, "and there were burns from the exhaust gasses inside the mouth."

"What then are the possibilities—other than that the good doctor was, in fact, involved in the crime and (so to speak) 'went out and hanged himself' ? "

"Obviously, John, Arthur Heath was conducting optical research as a side line. He may or may not have stumbled onto the principles for creating the machine. Whether he had or not, however, when I mentioned to him last night that he stood convicted except for a dead dog and a glass bead, he would hardly have avoided putting two and two together. He knew of someone else who had a supply of glass beads. That was the cause of last night's altercation. But as for the how of the murder, aside from the possibility of hypnosis, I can think of almost nothing."

"One doesn't just start dangling a watch fob in front of a raging bull," I noted with irony. "And who's got a pocket watch these days, anyway?"

"Hypnosis is unlikely," Geoffrey conceded. "But it is not out of the question. Any such control would have to spring from a post-hypnotic suggestion. And directors of secret projects do not go around allowing themselves to be put into a suggestible state. But it can be done."

"How?"

"By either beginning with drugs and switching to non-drug techniques, or by hypnotizing Heath in his sleep."

"But surely the latter is impossible," I stated with conviction.

"No, not at all. When I was a teenager, and pretty much a pagan, I did exactly that to a fellow. He got up and started walking before he awoke."

"But consider the problems. The man's wife would assuredly be sleeping in the same room."

"Oh to be sure, there are difficulties." Geoffrey stroked his goatee as he spoke. "But they are lessened if she is a heavy sleeper. And they are removed altogether if she is drugged, sleeps in another room, or is the thief herself—and a murderess."

"Weston, surely you don't believe that she could have killed him!"

"I have formed no opinion as yet," he assured me. "Her slight build is against it—unless there was an accomplice."

"Has she the technical training to put together the invisibility bullet?"

"That, of course, is a question—unless again she did not act alone."

"You said," I reminded him, "that outside of hypnosis you could think of *almost* no other method for carrying off the killing. Is there another?"

"John, do you believe in the existence of demons?"

"Why . . . yes," I answered, "I suppose I do."

"Could they drive a man to suicide?"

I left the question unanswered, and the two of us ascended the cellar stairs. As we reached the first floor hall, we could see the body being removed through the front door. We, however, turned to the rear in order to have one last chat with Susanna Heath. We found her on the porch. I had an idea what Geoffrey was going to ask. And I was not disappointed.

"Mrs. Heath," he greeted her, "I'm sorry to bother you again. But I have one or two questions before we go."

"It's no trouble at all," she assured us.

"Have you," he asked, "worked with your husband enough to be able to explain some of his experiments to us?"

"Gracious no. Arthur never even discussed that sort of thing with me. You see, Mr. Weston, I'm afraid I've never gone beyond preparatory school. When we were married, I dropped out so that I could help put Arthur through."

"Every man," Geoffrey responded gallantly, "should have a wife as self-sacrificing as you."

"Thank you."

"If the equipment downstairs is paid for, I'd like to make you an offer for some of it."

"Arthur always paid cash when he made purchases,"

Susanna replied with a smile. "But I think we'll save it for when Peter is a little older."

"Then I have only one further question," Weston concluded. "I presume that you and your husband slept in the same room. Did you hear him get up and leave—and if so, when?"

"I'm afraid I can't help you there. We have a double bed, but I don't know when he left. I heard some voices, but I can't tell you the time. I didn't get up until . . . until . . . " Her voice broke and she began sobbing.

"Yes, I understand," Geoffrey reassured her. "You needn't go on. Might I speak with your son for a moment?"

"Please do. He's still over there pruning." Tears were trickling down her cheeks.

We left Mrs. Heath and strolled out under the maples toward a ladder sticking up into a tree at the far end of the yard. As we neared our destination, we heard whistled strains of "God Save the Queen" coming from the topmost branches. I called out, I'm afraid, a bit bruskly. It did not seem the time for whistling.

"I say! You up there. Are you Peter Heath?"

"What's it to you?"

"We would like to speak with you about the death of your father."

A rustling of leaves was our only answer. In a moment legs dangled from the lower limbs and Peter Heath came down the ladder. His youthful features and long blond hair glowed in the morning sun. He greeted us with a smile.

"My foster father, sir—though people say I look a lot like him. Please forgive my bad manners. I was in the middle of sawing a branch. May I help you?"

"Indeed you may," I replied. "We would be most interested in knowing if you heard anything at all last night—before the shot, that is."

"I didn't even hear the shot, Mr. . . . "

"Taylor. John Taylor."

"I'm a very heavy sleeper, Mr. Taylor. I didn't know anything of the ghastly affair until Mother aroused me."

At this point Geoffrey took over the questioning.

"Can you tell us something," he asked, "of your father's experiments?"

"I'm sorry, but I don't know very much about that, either. You must already know that he's a biochemist. And he enjoyed tinkering around with that box in the basement. That's about all the information I have."

"Did he work alone?" Geoffrey probed.

"Usually. Sometimes Niles lent a hand."

"And what are your plans now?"

"I suppose I'll continue school as long as our savings last."

"What of insurance?"

"Since it was suicide, Mr. . . . "

"Weston."

"Since it was suicide, I don't suppose that the insurance will be paid."

"You believe, then, that it was a suicide?"

"Don't you, Mr. Weston?"

"One never knows, my boy."

"Well, if it was murder," Peter declared with conviction, "I hope you catch whoever did it. May I continue with my work now?"

"Oh, we wouldn't dream of detaining you," I interjected.

Without another word, Peter climbed the ladder once again. We made our way around the living room side of the house. Weston checked each flower bed on the off chance that there might be a footprint. Upon reaching the front, we walked down the street to our Mercedes and sped off toward Pinehurst Laboratory. As we drove toward Dorking, I made only one comment.

"Imagine whistling "God Save the Queen" on the day of your father's murder! What do you make of that?"

Weston's answer was curt.

"The young, it seems, have no concept of death."

CHAPTER 5

Atman

As we neared the Pinehurst facilities, Weston slowed the station wagon to a crawl and began looking for tire tracks at the side of the road. There had been no rain since the robbery. A quarter of a mile from the fence, our efforts were rewarded. My partner pointed off to the left.

"Look over there, old boy. We may have hit onto something."

We stopped on the asphalt and walked to the spot just beyond us where a vehicle had left the road. Weston was soon bending over—making a detailed examination. I returned to the car for my case and came back in a short while with a bucket of just-mixed plaster.

"I hope I haven't jumped the gun by preparing the batter," I apologized. "After all, there have been a good many police cars through here in the last few hours."

"I think not," Geoffrey reassured me. "The police would have taken better care of their tires. These are decidedly worn. Furthermore, this is just where one would park if he did not wish to be seen by a guard at the gate. And I believe that we have here impressions from a small truck. A pickup would have been needed to transport the bullet. We may be closing in on the thief—if, that is, the truck was not stolen and if its tires have not been replaced."

The casts took only a few moments to harden and be removed. With them safely in the back of the wagon, I drove the short distance to the gate. Geoffrey followed on foot—stopping now and again to peer at the dirt on the side of the road. I had been chatting for some time with the day guard—a youngish chap named Hollingswood—when Weston finally made his meandering way to the fence. He cast about for a distance of some twenty yards in every direction from the gate. At last satisfied, he took notice of us.

"Well, John, I see you've been passing the time profitably." He came over and shook the guard's hand. "To whom do I owe the pleasure?"

"This," I explained, "is Tim Hollingswood. Tim, I'd like you to meet my colleague, Geoffrey Weston."

"Good to meet you, sir," the guard responded. "Mr. Taylor tells me you're helping with the investigation.

"I'm doing my best."

"This is a queer enough affair," Tim observed. "Do you have any leads?"

"One or two. I'm not at liberty as yet to say just what they are. Have you two managed to light any candles of knowledge?"

"We are," I confided, "still quite in the dark. The thief could be anyone. Mr. Hollingswood tells me, though, that not very many pickups pass through these gates. Niles Gilbert has one. So does Alfred Bester. And there's a Janice Ragland."

"What about Heath's family?"

"Heath owned two MG's," Hollingswood volunteered. "One was used by his son. I know that because sometimes the young Mr. Heath would stop by here on an errand. It wasn't much of a car, though. I fancy it spent nearly as much time in the shop as on the road."

"And what of Mary Starling?" Weston continued.

"She drove an Opel—when she drove. But Niles Gilbert has been bringing her to work a lot lately."

"You've been of great assistance," my partner flattered. "We'd best be on our way now, but I may have some further questions to ask you later."

"Any time, sir. Just say the word."

Geoffrey and I climbed into the Mercedes. The guard opened the gate, and we entered the grounds. As we drove, I asked Geoffrey about his searches by the road. I learned that the thief had left some smudged impressions which hinted at being made by tennis shoes. They probably fit a medium-sized foot. But that was all. The markings were so indistinct that they were of little value. Weston, of course, had taken pictures with his pocket camera.

Our motorcar soon slid into a parking space next to the main laboratory building. As we walked toward the front entrance, Weston and I stopped to inspect the tires of the three pickups in the lot. None had treads that matched the tracks by the road.

The guard at the gate must have signaled to the laboratories, for a gentleman came bounding through the door almost as we reached it. In his haste he nearly bowled me over.

"Dear me!" he exclaimed. "I'm so sorry! You must be one of the detective fellows. Whatever is happening here? I hope you can find out who's responsible. In our eighteen-year history we've never had anything like this happen." As he was speaking, our somewhat rotund delegation of one straightened my coat. He followed his actions with all due sputtering and apology.

Weston, all the while, was looking with disdain upon the bureaucratic pomp of the man. Now my partner spoke—rescuing me from the clutches of gratitude.

"Get hold of yourself," he ordered. "We'll do all we can to solve the case. But who *are* you, anyway?"

"Oh, excuse me." Our host lost his hyperactivity— almost like a windup toy with its spring running down. "How forgetful of me. Of course you wouldn't know." The man adjusted his tie. "I'm Charles Woodward. I'm afraid I don't get around here much—am on the board, you see. But what with last night's tragic, tragic . . . ah accident, I've been asked to take over for poor Arthur— just until we can find a permanent replacement, you understand."

"And," Geoffrey replied, "just what are your duties insofar as we are concerned?"

"Why, to arrange for your interviews. Inspector Twigg told me that there would be a couple of detectives dropping by this morning to speak with the employees."

"Let's get on with it then, without delay," Weston suggested. He now consulted a note pad upon which I had scribbled some names during our drive. "I would like to speak with Albert Post, Niles Gilbert, James Smyth, and with a young lady named Mary Starling. I presume you have an office available for us to use during the questioning?"

"Yes, of course," the new director bubbled. "Ah . . . there is one thing, though. Mr. Post is not here."

"Oh?"

"He's been in the hospital for three weeks—is in a cast from the waist down. A motorway accident. Terrible thing . . ."

"Yes, indeed," Weston sympathized. "And the others?"

"There's no problem on that account," Charles Woodward assured us. "If you'll follow me, I'll show you gentlemen to our administrative offices. We'll page Niles from there on the intercom—that is, if he's the one you would like to interrogate first."

He was. When we arrived at the offices, Woodward instructed his secretary to call in the staff members one at a time. He then escorted us into the inner office.

"Do you wish me to remain during questioning?" he asked hopefully.

"You needn't bother," Weston replied. "We've already taken up quite enough of your time. There is something you might do to help us, though. Would you happen to know who owns the foreign pickup out in the parking lot?"

"No. But I can have the information for you in a few moments."

He left, rather importantly, on his errand. As the door closed behind him, I sat down in a sumptuously padded chair and waited a decent interval before speaking.

"Did you just ask him about the truck to keep him busy, or did I miss something?"

"Do I have to answer that either/or?" Weston was smiling. He leaned back in the swivel chair and put his hands behind his head. "Didn't you notice that the wheel base of that Ford matches the distance between those tracks at the side of the road? And its tires are so new that the rubber strings are still on the tread."

As he was still speaking, the door opened and the secretary announced that Niles Gilbert had arrived. Niles himself was just a step or two behind the young lady. He was an imposing figure of a man—well over six feet tall and weighing at least sixteen stone. Bushy, black eyebrows, a bald dome, and penetrating eyes combined to paint a rather extraordinary picture. Standing beside the secretary, he looked positively brutish. My friend, however, seemed not to notice.

"Please have a seat," Geoffrey invited. "We're sorry to have to call you away from your work, Mr. Gilbert. But we shan't detain you long."

"I certainly hope not . . . is it 'Inspector'? My time is of considerable value."

"I'm sure it is. May I introduce myself? I'm Geoffrey Weston. My colleague over there is John Taylor. Now, sir, let's get on with the questioning."

"That suits me." The scientist remained standing.

"Where were you," Geoffrey began, "the night before last between midnight and two in the morning?"

"You must be joking? Asleep in bed, of course."

"And at six o'clock this morning?"

"The same. And, in case you're wondering, I'm not married. You have only my word for where I was."

"That, Mr. Gilbert, is to your credit. It is invariably the guilty man who has the best alibi." Weston fixed his eyes upon our guest. "By the way, is that Ford in the parking lot yours?"

"Why, yes. How did you know?"

"I didn't. But it seemed likely that a man of your size would select what he drives with an eye toward head room. Are you satisfied with the pickup's performance?"

"Quite satisfied, thank you." Niles Gilbert smiled sardonically. "I'm touched that you would be so interested in my comfort."

"Not only in your comfort," Geoffrey assured him. "In your safety. How long has it been since you changed the tires on your truck?"

"Now there you've got me. It's been several months. I hope you're not going to give me a ticket."

"That's a little out of my line," Geoffrey admitted. "Does anyone besides yourself have a key to the vehicle?"

"Mr. Weston, I've already told you I'm a bachelor. *I* drive the pickup—period. But what's all this interest in the Ford about, anyway?"

Weston brushed aside the question. "I understand that you practice a form of meditation."

"Yes. I am seeking to more fully experience my unity with Atman—the soul of Brahmana. But surely that is of no concern to you."

"You would be amazed at my interests."

"I already am," Niles conceded.

"You are a Hindu?"

"I am."

"Have you," Geoffrey asked, "ever initiated Dr. Heath into the discipline of yoga?"

"I'm not aware that that's a crime. But the answer's no. We talked about it. It would have helped him—he needed to relax. But Arthur was a materialist. To him it was all so much rubbish. His son has shown some interest, but the old man was very closed minded."

"And you're not?"

"I don't believe so," the scientist considered. "As far as I'm concerned, every religion is a reflection of truth."

"Even when some condemn all the others as being made up of lies?"

"There are many paradoxes in this universe, Inspector. In truth lies falsehood."

"By which statement you reflect the mental set of your religion. Anyone who stands for paradox stands for nothing.

"You are thinking with a Western mind," Niles suggested. "How can one really know anything? As Lao-tse has said: 'If when I was asleep I was a man dreaming I was a butterfly, how do I know when I am awake that I am not a butterfly dreaming I am a man?' ''

"If man is that stupid and knowledge that tenuous," Weston shot back, "then how could Lao-tse even know enough to ask the question? And how could you credit your own comment with having any worth? If you doubt that man can have knowledge, then you must doubt your doubt—for it purports to be a sort of knowledge. Really, Mr. Gilbert, you are a scientist—not a dreamer. And you yourself are a Westerner."

"In body. But I am sick of the smug pride of the West."

"Sir, if you believe every group's beliefs to be equally true and equally an illusion, then do you condone the human sacrifice practiced by some? Would you see anything wrong, for example, with the sacrifice of Arthur Heath?"

"Are you accusing me of murder?" Niles Gilbert retorted.

"Are you evading the question?" Geoffrey asked.

"No, of course not."

"Then," Weston advised, "I'd like to know if you regard murder as evil."

"Surely you realize that Hindus hold all life to be sacred. There is truth and falsehood in all religion, but murder is certainly a part of the error in those religions which practice it." At this point in the conversation, Niles finally sat down. His stay was evidently a little longer than he had expected.

"But isn't it true," Weston continued, "that you believe in a being who is the great ALL—from whose essence the universe springs?"

"That is essentially correct."

"A bad pun, Mr. Gilbert. And do you consider everyone to be a part of this 'great ALL'? "

"I do."

"Then," Geoffrey concluded, "for you the murderer, rapist, and prostitute are all a part of god. Your god is the source of both good *and evil.* How can there be any real difference between the two as far as you are concerned?"

Niles looked steadily at my partner.

"I'd prefer not to answer that."

"Mr. Gilbert," Weston concluded, "you are trapped in a monster. Have you been doing its 'good evil'? Did you kill Arthur Heath?"

"I most certainly did not," the scientist replied emphatically. "Until listening to you, I didn't even know that he was murdered."

"He was. Was it wrong?"

"He . . . He was my friend."

"That's not what I asked," Geoffrey reminded him. "Is your non-violence a pose to cover up an amoral murder?"

"I've already answered that," Niles Gilbert shot back. "I'm not going to sit here and be accused of killing my best friend."

"Ah, but what is friendship? Surely it is only an illusion—a projection of an impersonal ground of being."

"You're making sport of me," Niles responded icily.

"Not of you," my partner corrected him. "Of your ideas."

"And what have you that's better?" the scientist countered.

"I believe personally that God made man in His image but not as a mere projection of himself. Man chose to disobey. God judged the evil. In that way I can understand pain and sin without losing respect for God."

"You explain pain," Niles objected, "at the expense

of rejecting man's unity with the universe. I see in what you say only alienation and despair."

"You see only what you want to see," Geoffrey chided. "Surely I don't have to tell you that the central doctrine of Christianity is that a Saviour came to earth and made payment for sins. Unity with God is restored to the person who places his trust in Christ. But it is not a unity that causes a loss of identity."

"Oh, yes, Jesus Christ. You believe that He is God?"

"I do," Weston declared.

"You accept the Trinity?"

"Yes."

"Then," Niles Gilbert concluded triumphantly, "your own system is based on three being one—a paradox. As you yourself said: 'Anyone who stands for paradox stands for nothing.' "

"But you're changing the definition of paradox," Weston declared. 'Good' and 'evil' are opposites by definition. 'Three,' however, is not the opposite of 'one.' 'Zero' is."

"Oh, come now," Niles chuckled, "three equals one?"

"And in high school," Geoffrey reminded him, "didn't you compute that 'one' equals 'two'?"

"You're getting desperate, Weston. That was a mere game."

"Not at all desperate," Geoffrey insisted. "Light is made of particles. Light is made of waves. One substance under given conditions can be solid, liquid, and gas in the same container at the same time at the same temperature. The universe is infinite. The universe is circular. Some paradoxes are such because they are logically impossible—a collection of contradictory opposites. Your system is based on that kind of animal. But other paradoxes are only apparent. They exist only because they stand beyond man's ability to understand. To an infinite mind they are reasonable. What is the logic, Niles, in the tenth dimension? You're considering 'three' and 'one' only as three-dimensional terms. But what do the words mean to a Being who exists equally in all dimensions?

"Since my mind is not infinite," Niles remarked drolly, "I'll let that question pass. But let me point out that I consider 'good' and 'evil' to be terms of human invention—nothing more. If that is so, then neither really exists, and my religion produces no paradox."

"At least not at that point. But, Niles, can you live without the distinction between good and evil? Your friend died. Was that neutral? You conduct experiments. Are you in search of results that are morally meaningless? If so, why go to the bother of expending the effort? Man *cannot* operate in a moral vacuum. And for morality to have *any* meaning, there must be an absolute criterion for measurement. A milligram is a milligram is a milligram, or you could never mix chemicals. And good is good is good, or you have no motive for mixing."

"There is always salary."

"Which is good or evil?" Weston prompted.

"Which is neither."

"Then why do you work?"

"Because I wish to."

"And why do you wish to?"

"That," the scientist concluded, "is an existential reality which I cannot convey to you."

"So now," Geoffrey accused, "you flee the field of battle and debate into the solipsistic confines of your own mind."

"At least as effective a strategy," Niles retorted, "as appealing to an infinite mind in order to deliver yourself from a paradox. And I was not aware that I had been debating."

"You certainly sounded like it. And aren't you fleeing?"

"I'm terminating the conversation."

"Which amounts to the same thing," Geoffrey declared.

"Mr. Weston," Niles observed, "you don't sound like any Scotland Yard detective to me. Who are you?"

"I wasn't aware that I had said anything about being from the Yard."

"You intimated as much," the scientist charged.

"No," Weston corrected him, "it was you who made the suggestion. I'm a consulting detective, actually. Your best friend called me into the case at the suggestion of a Yard detective."

Niles Gilbert stood up and stretched.

"It appears," he declared, "that I have been wasting my time. If I had known that you were unofficial, I would have walked out ten minutes ago."

"How fortunate then," Geoffrey commented dryly, "that you made the error. As it happens, I'm almost down to my last question."

"And that's as far as you will go."

Geoffrey seemed not to have heard.

"You are a Hindu," he continued. "Your respect for life prohibits you from even killing sick and starving cows. How, then, do you rationalize taking part in experiments in genetic engineering?"

I must admit that I myself was startled by Geoffrey's final assault. But my reaction was as nothing compared with that of Niles Gilbert. It was as though an epee had pierced his heart. His face flushed. His voice, hardly more than a whisper, cracked as he replied.

"How . . . How did you . . . find out?"

"I found out," Weston declared, "by looking at your face this very moment. I had surmised as much, however, from the interesting collection of degrees held by members of the staff, and from the nature of the underlining in Heath's home library. How very human to shroud research in secrecy but then to leave books on genetics, cell structure, and microsurgery on (as it were) public display!"

"You mustn't say a word of this to anyone," Niles cautioned. "It would mean our ruin. If the press should get hold of it, the public would . . . would . . . "

"Yes, I quite understand." Geoffrey folded his hands in front of him and spoke reassuringly. "John and I are both capable of keeping our lips closed. I take it that your experiments involve more than, say, altering viruses to give them disease-fighting properties. Offhand, I can think of only two activities which would arouse such animosity from the public. Would you care to tell me which it is?"

"I would not."

"I didn't think you would. Have you decided, Niles, that you are the monster?"

"I don't know."

"And that," Geoffrey concluded, "is the first intelligent thing you've said since you came in here. I have all the information I need. You are free to go now."

"Thank you."

Niles strode to the door and had his hand to the knob when Geoffrey's voice cut the air again.

"By the way, have you given anyone driving lessons during the last few months or loaned out your house key?"

The scientist half turned toward us.

"I don't loan out keys. But I have given a lesson or two."

"To whom?"

"I don't really see what business it is of yours."

"Then," Weston suggested, "you refuse to answer?"

"I . . . No, I'll answer. All you have to do is ask them, anyway. I taught Mary (that's Mary Starling), and Susan and Peter Heath. Good day."

Niles Gilbert opened the door and escaped—slamming it closed behind him. He quite obviously did not want to chance being asked any further questions.

I had been so engrossed in the conversation between the two that I had tensed up. Now I leaned back into soft padding and let out a deep breath.

"Weston," I spoke admiringly, "you have the pluck of a London cabby. A man seemingly reacts to your interrogation by blowing his brains out, and not half a day later you ask the same kind of questions to his best friend. And with what results! We'll have Gilbert in the dock before very long, unless I miss my guess."

"Why do you think so?"

"Where shall I begin?" I marked off the reasons on my fingers. "He lied to us about the tires. He is an expert in hypnotic states. The chap is amoral. He knows his way around both the laboratories and Heath's house. He has no alibi. And he's done work with the beads."

"He also is a friend of Mrs. Heath," Geoffrey filled in. "But I don't think he's either a thief or a murderer."

"You don't?" I asked with a good bit of surprise.

"At this stage I'm not certain. But it seems to me that his story about the tires was a little too clumsy to be false. He could have invented a better lie."

"Yet surely," I considered, "if he had told us he'd bought new tires, we would have asked where. Then we might have recovered the trade-ins with the incriminating treads."

"Not if the present tires are stolen," Geoffrey pointed out.

"Stolen?"

"Didn't you notice that they are two-ply tires made for a motorcar? Surely he wouldn't have *purchased* anything that light."

"Then that settles it," I reasoned. "He could hardly say: 'No, my tires are new. I stole them just yesterday.' So he acted as though he didn't know anything about the exchange."

"But why would he risk robbery when all he had to do was buy the tires and then either claim that he hadn't or that he couldn't remember where he had made the purchase? No, I think it's more likely that someone else used the pickup and then changed tires."

"If anyone besides Gilbert used the truck," I objected, "why would he bother with making the switch?"

"Why indeed?" Geoffrey drummed his fingers on the desk. "But why would Niles steal the papers. He was already privy to the bulk of the information they contained. And he is only theoretically immoral. I think at least the memory of personal honour keeps him fairly honest. And did you notice his height?"

"What's that got to do with anything?"

"Simply that the man is so enormous that if you stuffed him into the bullet—allowing a foot of overhead for the projection equipment—the invisibility machine would have to be too tall to fit through any of the doors in this building. It could not have reached the safe!"

"But," I insisted, "there could have been an accomplice."

"That's a possibility. But an accomplice could supply Mr. Gilbert with an alibi—which he doesn't have."

"We don't know that he has one. He may be holding it in reserve. And remember that he's a Hindu. He might have taken the papers in order to preserve life."

"Or," Geoffrey theorized, "perhaps another person used the truck—someone closely enough associated with Niles Gilbert so that the thief felt it necessary to hide the fact that it was Gilbert's pickup that had been used."

Our speculations were interrupted as the door opened and a tired little man walked in and extended his hand to us. He introduced himself as James Smyth and took the seat offered to him. Geoffrey began the questioning.

"Mr. Smyth, I was very impressed with your personnel file. You are a man of unusual intelligence."

"Thank you."

"Are you content here at Pinehurst Laboratory?"

"Oh, most assuredly."

"You don't," Weston suggested, "feel that you are being paid somewhat less than you deserve?"

"No, not at all."

"Do you know of any employees who are discontented?"

James Smyth thought for a moment.

"I honestly don't know of anyone. We are a happy family here."

"But," Geoffrey reminded him, "there's theft and perhaps murder in the family. Don't you think that odd?"

"I credit the job to an outsider."

Weston gazed sternly across the desk.

"Where were you, Mr. Smyth, on these last two nights?"

"At the time of the excitements?"

"Yes."

"Sleeping."

"Were there any witnesses," my partner asked.

"My wife. That is, she was with me."

"But neither of you was awake?"

"No."

"Thank you very much for your cooperation. If I think of anything further to ask, I'll let you know."

That ended our second interview. James Smyth took leave of us, and five minutes later Mary Starling entered. She seemed annoyed.

"Which one of you is the dreadful Mr. Weston?"

Geoffrey answered with a slight bowing gesture.

"I am, I must admit, Weston. But I'm not familiar with the adjective."

"You're a horrid man," she accused. "What gives you the right to pry into people's private affairs and preach to them?"

"The same law that gives you the right to condemn me for it. I see you have been speaking with Niles."

"Yes, I have. And he told me what to expect from you."

"Fascinating." Geoffrey smiled. "You are, then, very close to Niles."

"We're going to be married," she confessed.

"Where were you the night before last between midnight and two in the morning?"

"I was with Niles."

"Thank you very much, Miss Starling. That will be all."

"It will?" She seemed surprised.

"Yes, indeed. You're free to go—that is, unless you'd like to stay longer."

"Oh no!"

"Then have a good day. Say hello to Niles for me."

With a somewhat dazed expression on her face, Mary Starling walked through the doorway. We could hear her high heels clicking down the hall. When Geoffrey and I left the inner office, we were met by the secretary. She handed us a note that Charles Woodward had left in her charge. I tore open the envelope and deciphered the pretentious swirls: "The vehicle is the property of a Mister Niles Gilbert."

C.W.

CHAPTER 6

The Hows of Yogacide

Before leaving the front gate, Geoffrey stopped to ask young Hollingswood who (besides the police, guards, ourselves, and Arthur Heath) had entered the grounds yesterday. We learned that Niles had come to work to monitor an experiment then in progress. Peter Heath had brought his father some lunch. With that knowledge under our belts we sped into the countryside—our station wagon hurrying purposefully to somewhere.

"Is it going to be to Reigate or London?" I asked.

"Oh, I fancy to Reigate," Weston responded. "I want to have a look at Mr. Gilbert's house before he returns from work."

"Hadn't we better get in touch with Twigg, then, so he can arrange the papers?"

"There's no time, John. If we don't get into that house immediately, I'm virtually certain that somebody else is going to die tonight."

"You're finally convinced then of Gilbert's guilt," I ventured. "It certainly was a bit much when his fiancée came up with that alibi for him."

"I'm sure of only one thing," he objected. "There'll

be another murder tonight in Reigate unless we stop it."

We rode on in silence. Geoffrey was in another of his theatrical moods, and it was useless to try to get any information out of him. I'd find out soon enough what he had in mind. We slowed at the Reigate city limits and turned onto a side street. A few blocks further on we drove by the home of the late Dr. Heath. We parked two blocks down the street and then walked back to Gilbert's house—three lots over from the scene of last night's murder.

"You check the right side," Geoffrey instructed. "I'll take the left. Let me know if you find a window ajar."

There were no windows cracked open. The house, an austere woodframe structure with gables, was locked up tightly. Weston and I met in the backyard. As he came into view, I shook my head. But he didn't seem particularly disturbed.

"Well," my partner declared with aplomb, "there's nothing for it but to use the back door like any self-respecting guest. At moments like this I always think of Rahab protecting the spies."

He took a set of skeleton keys from his pocket and tried them one at a time in the lock. The third key opened the door, and we calmly stepped inside. Weston handed me a pair of gloves to put on.

"I want you to look for a gun," he explained. "The man may not have one. He's big enough that he may depend on his fists. If so, so much the worse. We can't do anything about the cutlery."

We searched the house from top to bottom. I opened drawer after drawer—always being careful to leave everything just as it had been. Weston explored closets, punched pillows, and checked under beds. In all we found two pistols—a revolver and an automatic. They were ancient but serviceable. And both were loaded.

Geoffrey and I carefully removed the slug from each bullet, along with a portion of the powder. I took a few sheets of toilet tissue from the bathroom, and we used it as tamping to hold the powder in place in the casings. We reloaded the guns with the blanks and brushed the leavings into an envelope which I initialed and placed in my pocket. Weston returned the revolver to a drawer of the roll-top desk in the living room. I placed the automatic in a bureau in Gilbert's bedroom. As I came down the stairs, Geoffrey greeted me in a low voice.

"We'd best get out of here quickly. We're not dressed for entertaining visitors. And pray that there's no third gun."

We walked out the back door as bold as brass. Weston locked up and returned the keys to his pocket with a flourish. The two of us walked down the driveway at the side of the house and turned down the street. As we strode toward the car, I spoke more to myself than to Geoffrey.

"Do you suppose anybody's seen us?"

"If they have," he replied, "they probably think we are a couple of old fraternity brothers that Niles has invited over for a few days. At least let's hope so."

We got in the car and were about to pull away from the curb when we saw a police cruiser coming up the street toward us. As it neared, the driver slowed. Then we heard a shout.

"Hello there. Fancy meeting you here, Weston!"

It was Inspector Twigg. Geoffrey opened the door to our wagon and went over to have a few words with him. I could hear them talking.

"Well, well, Inspector. What brings you back this way?"

"I might ask you the same. You've missed the house by a good two blocks. Not very good for the supersleuth! Or are you trying to keep others from knowing you're skulking about? Me, for instance?"

"Oh, not at all,Filbert. I'm more than happy to see you—could have done with your help a while ago, in fact."

Inspector Twigg winced at the mention of his first name. Very few knew he even had it. And, except for Geoffrey, none dared use it.

"Well," the Inspector informed him, "as it happens I'm somewhat pleased to see you, too. I have some information which you might find of interest. There was nothing out of the ordinary in Heath's body—so far as we can as yet tell. There was no anaesthetic. We found no hallucinogen. He had not been drinking. There was no sodium pentothal. Case closed. The man simply killed himself. It happens every day. Maybe he had something to hide. I understand from what Niles Gilbert says that you think it was murder."

"One hears stories, doesn't one."

"Are you holding anything back from me?" Twigg pressed. "Is there *any* physical evidence that points to murder?"

"None," Weston stated decisively.

"Then I wish you'd get on to solving the theft and stop exciting the staff at Pinehurst."

The Inspector did not seem happy at all.

"Do you have anything on the dog autopsy yet?" Geoffrey reminded him.

"Oh, yes indeed. He died of exactly the same thing that killed Dr. Heath—a bullet in the brain. And he had exactly the same chemicals in him—BLOOD. You've had two goals scored on you, Weston. Better luck next time."

"Doesn't it strike you as significant that both the dog and the man died in a similar manner?"

"In a similar manner!" Twigg bellowed. "One was shot. The other shot himself."

"Yet both had the markings of suicides."

"Not so," the Inspector disagreed. "Both *were* suicides. They could have been nothing else. You're letting your flair for the bizarre dull your senses, man!"

"Twigg, have there been any large thefts of television supplies recently?"

"I don't know. Would you like me to look into the matter for you?"

"If you would."

"I'll see what I can do," the Inspector promised. "And now, if you have no further requests . . ."

"I'm quite through."

"Have a good hunt."

Twigg pushed his Austin into gear and left Weston standing in the road. A moment later my colleague and I were driving in the opposite direction from that taken by the police car. We turned a corner and pulled into a service station for some petrol. As the attendant filled the tank, Geoffrey visited a pay phone and leafed through the directory. He returned in two minutes—whistling and munching on some peanuts. We entered traffic once again and continued up the same road for several blocks. Then we parked in front of a large showroom. A sign on the top of the building announced that domestic and imported Fords were available to all interested buyers. Weston nudged me.

"Let's take a look at some new cars. I'm particularly interested in one which may come equipped with some rather unusual tires."

We stepped into the showroom and were met by a salesman.

"May I help you, gentlemen?"

"Why, yes, indeed," I replied. "We would like to see

the full assortment of your new models."

"Certainly, sir. Have a look about the showroom, and let me know if you need assistance."

Weston had already surveyed the glistening display room with a critical eye. We would not find what we wanted here. But then we had hardly expected to. My partner looked about in an obvious manner.

"Do you have anything other than these? In a back lot perhaps?"

"Oh, certainly, sir." The salesman's voice oozed charm. "Just follow me out that door, and I'll show you the full selection."

"Thank you," I replied, "but we can find the way ourselves."

"As you wish."

We swept past the man and pushed through the back door. An acre and a half of glistening, fake chrome met our gaze. My enthusiasm deflated a bit. With that jungle of cars to be inspected, I suddenly had the sickening feeling that our burglar had only stolen spares. Or we might be in the wrong lot entirely. The location of the dealership, at least, was in our favor. I hoped Geoffrey was right in believing this the only place in town that sold the right brand. We split up and began walking up and down rows. Halfway up my third row, I found a model with the new electric engine. Its accessories were not nearly so up-to-date.

"Have a look here," I called out.

In a matter of seconds Geoffrey had reached my side and bent down to study the treads. I held my torch so he could see clearly in the shadows. It didn't take long for a verdict. Satisfied, Weston looked up.

"There's no room for doubt. These are the tires. It's an off chance, but dust them—at least as much as you can get to with them still on the car."

I pulled a brush and a small can of powder from my kit and began to work. Geoffrey, meanwhile, scrutinized the ground around the vehicle. Unfortunately the lot was paved with asphalt. So he had to content himself with taking pictures of the car and tires with his pocket flash. He then walked the perimeter of the lot—inspecting the high fence surrounding it. The gate was locked. There were no pieces of cloth snagged on the top. At one point, he told me later, six wire points at the top of the fence had been bent over. Someone had climbed it.

While Geoffrey did his part, I carefully spread the white powder on the rubber and brushed it off again—inch by inch. The salesman must have been curious at our delay. I could hear him several cars away talking with Geoffrey about the merits of a particular Thunderbird. Finally I finished. As I had suspected, the results were negative. Our thief was an expert. He was not likely to slip up on so simple a matter. Nor had he. When I stood up, the salesman's back was to me. I walked over in their direction and rather startled the man by speaking.

"I'm afraid I've found nothing, Geoffrey. Absolutely nothing."

"Somehow I didn't think you would, old chap." Weston took my cue. "You know they don't make automobiles the way they used to. Not at all."

The salesman was obviously crestfallen. But he eased gamely into his sales talk.

"Actually, this year's models are the best we've ever—"

"No, I'm sorry, young fellow," my partner interrupted. "It's just a case of cheaper materials and shoddier workmanship. It seems every year there's more plastic. One of these days the motor won't even be metal. But I have a friend who will, I believe, be interested in one of your cars in the morning."

"Thank you for recommending us." The man looked puzzled.

"Think nothing of it," Weston answered suavely. "It's the least we can do. I believe you'll turn a profit from his call."

We walked back through the showroom and out the front door. The salesman stood where we left him—no doubt still wondering why we would hate his automobiles but still put in a good word about them to someone. I was doing some wondering myself about that time. Why hadn't Geoffrey simply told the chap at Exeter Ford that there'd been a robbery? We would, after all, be in a real pickle if the evidence should disappear before we reported it.

As we drove down Southampton Street towards the motorway, I thought the matter through. My friend had something planned for tonight. He didn't want to be thrown off schedule by having the police question us. That much was clear. But why not report and run, so to speak? Niles Gilbert would be taken in custody, and we could all breathe easier.

"You don't want him arrested, do you?" I thought out loud.

"Want who arrested?" Geoffrey had his bag of peanuts out again and was munching.

"Gilbert, of course."

Weston looked across at me in mock horror. "What, and spoil our evening?" He'd given me the opening I was waiting for.

"One part of that evening that I'm looking forward to is dinner," I declared hopefully. "You wouldn't be looking for a restaurant, would you?"

My companion chuckled. "That's the fastest bit of

gear changing I've heard in a long time."

"I don't have any peanuts," I defended myself.

"Have a few," Geoffrey offered.

"Nor do I like them," I reminded him.

I noticed with satisfaction that we were turning into the parking lot of an establishment known as THE LION AND CROWN. A blinking sign greeted me with the promise of "steak and onions."

"I discovered this place on a trip through here a few months ago," my partner explained. "It looks rather like it was built with a cookie cutter, but the food is decent."

So Geoffrey had been headed here all along.

The restaurant lived up to its billing. The waitress was a bit long in coming to take our order, but all that was forgiven as I took my first bite. I even decided to avoid making any sarcastic remarks about the sheet-metal suits of armour in each corner.

"Weston, this is fabulous! It's been years since I've tasted beefsteak pudding this good."

"Wait until you get to the tipsy cake," he advised. "You'll never want to go anywhere else." He set about devouring his own plate of halibut Bristol.

"How's yours?" I asked.

"Magnifico!" He kissed his fingers in the Continental gesture of appreciation. "They've used real butter. The cheese is aged, and the mussels are fresh—instead of the other way around."

I speared another chunk of meat with my fork. "So much for stocking up with food, Geoff. What about the proverbial forty winks?"

"I'm afraid sleep will have to wait. We can always catch up on it when the case is solved."

I groaned.

"In fact," he continued mercilessly, "we won't have

time to return to Baker Street this evening. We will be conducting a stake-out of the Gilbert house."

I was not overjoyed at the prospect.

"Couldn't we leave that in Twigg's hands? He's got the men for it."

Geoffrey shook his head reproachfully. "The men, yes. But I want us to be the first ones into the place when the action starts."

"If the action starts," I corrected.

"Oh, it will."

"If it does," I lamented, "judging from past cases we'll be waiting until dawn before things get lively."

"Don't worry about that, John. If you lie still on the ground, dew won't form on the grass." His optimism evoked another groan.

"And when do we begin this stake-out?" I asked.

"We should be in position when Niles gets home from work. As nearly as I can figure, that gives us fifteen minutes to eat."

From that point on we chewed in silence. I was not about to mix conversation with food and leave a piece of unfinished steak on the plate. True to his word, in exactly a quarter hour Geoffrey rose to leave. I took care of the tip while he paid the check.

As we drove in the other direction down Southhampton, I suppressed the urge to ask him if he ever got tired. I already knew the answer: "Only between cases, John. Only between cases."

This time we parked around the corner and two blocks over from the Gilbert house. Since the road we were on dead-ended, we were not likely to have our car spotted by Twigg or by anyone else headed for or leaving the scene of last night's murder. Keeping ourselves out of sight until dark was, however, another matter. Weston pulled the curtains in the wagon and changed into coveralls. A mustache and a bucket of tempera paint completed his disguise. His was the easy part. Until the next hard rain, residents would find it illegal to park across the street from 1631 Chestnut Lane. We walked the two blocks, with Geoffrey cutting quite a figure. The mustache added some dash to his features—complementing the goatee. But that was more than offset by the bucket and brush that he was lugging. The disguise would have been more effective if he had shaved his chin.

When we reached Chestnut Lane, my partner crossed the street and walked up the block until he arrived at a spot opposite Niles Gilbert's home. He then dutifully opened the can and began painting a "no parking" stripe on the side of the gutter. I waited five minutes and then worked my way around to the back of the house. I hid behind a bush and hoped that no busybody in the house to my rear was staring at me through the window. I had no sooner settled down when a pickup pulled into the driveway. Niles was not alone. As he walked toward the house, I could see Mary Starling leaning on his arm. She was decidedly more chirp than roar at the moment. They entered the building arm in arm. I noted the time on my pad. In about an hour the two emerged again, laughing. They returned to the Ford and drove off.

Thus far the evening did not seem particularly menacing. At least the sun had finally set. I could feel a little more secure about not being seen. By now Weston had probably abandoned his masquerade and taken up a position behind some bush also. After all, not many painters paint in the dark. As night chill set in, I began to wish that I had brought along a jug of hot tea.

At ten after ten, headlights turned into the driveway. This time Niles was alone. I could hear him cursing as he tried the wrong key in the lock. Then there was a creaking sound. The kitchen light blazed to life—silhouetting him in the doorway. The door slammed. One by one the rear windows lit up. And I lay still and watched.

The silence became oppressive—relieved only by the call of a night bird or the drone of a passing motorist. Now and again a wisp of fog passed between myself and the house—lending a sinister cast to the old building. In my mind the house of the seven gables lived again. As I stared, my fancy pierced the walls in search of their secrets.

Weston was wrong. Dew *had* formed its droplets under me. I remembered an old copy of the *Express* lying on the back seat of the Mercedes. I could have kicked myself for not bringing it along to spread on the ground. Try as I might, I couldn't twist my body into any position that was comfortable.

With a start I forced myself to lie completely still. There was somebody out in the darkness. I hadn't heard a sound or seen any movement, but somehow I knew. I listened, hardly breathing, until my ears rang from the silence. Nothing. Then there it was—not a sound, but something else. A hideous slime seemed to be oozing at the edge of my consciousness. I felt utterly defiled—as though I'd been dipped into a cesspool. The yard was empty, and yet my chest now strained against a pressure that forced the air from my lungs. I closed my eyes. All of the sexual fantasies I'd ever had flashed irresistibly across my mind. In desperation I called out in a hoarse whisper: "HELP ME, JESUS! I CLAIM YOUR BLOOD!"

With a fluttering, the weight lifted. There was only silence—blessed silence. I was alone. According to my watch it was now eleven-thirty.

Three shots rang out. I got to my feet and began running toward the house. Halfway there, I tripped over a hose and nearly fell. But, regaining my balance, I put on a last burst of speed. Panting, I pushed my weight against the back door and broke through into the kitchen. No one was there. I hurried toward the living room. Even as I did, I could hear Weston smashing through the door. The two of us arrived in the living room at almost the same instant.

Seated cross-legged and erect on the middle of the rug, Niles Gilbert was crying softly. He wore flaired, oriental trousers—and nothing else. Even as we reached him, the pistol went off three more times in rapid succession. He was holding the end of the barrel to his temple—and he was chanting.

"I must lose myself and be one with Atman. I can't live without good . . . without good . . . without good. I can't . . . Mary, where is love? No love. No love. No good. No difference. Only darkness. And tears. And TEARS . . . And tears and . . . and . . . and . . . "

He squeezed the trigger again, but nothing happened. I grabbed the gun out of his hand and flung it aside. Weston began slapping him across the face.

"Wake up, man! Wake up! It's all over. There's good. There's love. There's truth." He punctuated each assurance with another slap. Slowly the glazed stare left Niles' eyes and he looked up at us. Although a giant of a man, he began sobbing uncontrollably. Weston placed his arm around his shoulder.

"Take it easy. It's all over now."

A welt was beginning to form on Gilbert's temple—burn marks from the powder. But he was otherwise unhurt. After a moment we helped him to his feet, and Weston led him upstairs. I closed the front and back doors and followed. With any luck it would take awhile for anyone to track down the source of the shots. Almost certainly Heath's house would be searched first. I hoped that the neighbors' confusion would give us a short time alone with Niles. As I entered the bedroom, the scientist was speaking.

" . . . was like a belt around my chest. And I heard whispers. Over and over they repeated your arguments against Atman. They became louder and louder, and I couldn't answer them. I only knew that I couldn't live without good. Without good there is nothing. They told me there was nothing. They reminded me again and again of the gun. There was no good. No evil. No purpose. I had to escape to blessed nothingness. I didn't want to. But . . . there was nothing else . . . " He began sobbing again.

"And did the voices," Weston asked, "mention anything of my alternative?"

"No. No, they didn't."

"And they never will. It is beyond them. And they hate it. Are you ready to surrender to the God-man?"

"Yes, I am," Niles replied soberly. "Without Him, what is there?"

"Do you still believe that 'good' and 'evil' are myths?"

"No. I see evil in myself."

Geoffrey looked him steadily in the eye.

"Then you are ready."

Niles Gilbert stifled a sob and prayed. As he did, the tears of a lifetime ran down his cheeks.

I could hear a pounding on the front door. So I left the two alone and went down to answer the knock. When I reached the landing, I could see that I was too late. A bobby was inside the door, and Twigg was just a step behind. Ours had not been the only stake-out tonight. The police had done a good job up the street. I hadn't seen them. Maybe something that Geoffrey had said had given Twigg second thoughts. As I continued toward them, I called out a greeting.

"Well, Inspector! Good to see you on the job—even if you were a couple of houses off. We've another corpse for you. But this one is alive. You won't find any drug in *him*, either. And, by the way, there's a certain Ford agency with some old tires . . ."

CHAPTER 7

The Room Beyond

The covers were delicious—luxurious. I stretched lazily in their warmth. "Ah, Baker Street! How satisfying you are! It's good to be home." I rolled over and closed my eyes again. But I could hear footfalls in the hallway. How well I knew their meaning! A second later Weston's voice twisted deftly through the keyhole.

"Up up, Taylor! There's a murderer to catch. And it's nearly eight o'clock. The stores will be opening soon, and we'll need to make some purchases."

I opened leaden eyelids and mumbled a reply. Something about the business districts burning to the ground, I believe. But I stumbled to my feet and got dressed. A little water splashed in my face half revived me. In the kitchen I found a cup of steaming, black coffee sitting at my place at the table.

"Well, well, there you are," Geoffrey beamed. "It's about time."

I grumbled under my breath and sipped the coffee—scalding my tongue in the process. After that I spooned and blew the brackish stuff. I swallowed in moody silence. Finally, when the last drop had been consumed, I looked up from the cup.

"What's for breakfast?" I asked. "And how did you know that Gilbert would try to make an end of it last night?"

Weston eyed my scowl impishly.

"Bacon and eggs, and I'll tell you while we eat."

Fortunately the pan was already sizzling, so there was not long to wait. Geoffrey, in his at-home moments, is an excellent cook. My own talents lean more toward the eating. I stuck a muffin in the toaster. My colleague slid a full plate in front of me, we said grace, and he took his place at the table. While I devoured what was before me, Weston (who snacks as he cooks) ate slowly and — between bites—explained his reasoning.

"It was no great deduction, actually, to realize that Niles Gilbert was marked as the next victim. I was certain of it as soon as he told me he owned the Ford. He was a physical link—the only one—with the murderer. And I could not see Heath's killer allowing any link to remain for even a moment longer than necessary. So I deliberately did with Gilbert what I had done with Heath—forcing him to see the inconsistencies at the end of his philosophy. That provided the murderer with the tool he needed for taking quick action. All he had to do was to force home those inconsistencies until Niles reached the breaking point. And, of course, Niles reached it. The yoga trance made it all the easier for the killer."

"But who," I stopped chewing to ask, "is the killer?"

"As to that, I have an idea. I believe I know the who and the how. But the why is just beyond my finger tips. For that we'll have to find out what's on the other side of that locked door in Heath's laboratory."

I whistled.

"And how do you propose to find that out?"

"All in good time, John. All in good time." He

fished a piece of paper out of his shirt pocket. "When we've finished breakfast and you wash the grease off your fingers, you may be interested in the contents of this shopping list." He turned his attention exclusively toward the scrambled eggs.

We got up from the table at eight-thirty. I had just enough time to reach the stores as they opened. Weston handed me the list. It was, to say the least, suggestive.

"So," I deduced, "you're going to construct an invisibility machine of your own. But won't your suggestions to the guards make it impossible for you to get in?"

"Oh, the entry won't be a problem. We're simply going to walk up the hall in sight of everyone. The machine will only be used once we're inside Heath's laboratory."

"And what of our integrity?"

"I don't see any difficulty there, John. We shall neither force entry into the laboratory nor into the room beyond. We won't steal anything. We'll simply investigate an area of the laboratory wall that has previously escaped our attention. We have been told not to open the door. We won't. We have been told not to enter the room behind it. We won't. We'll stay scrupulously within the limits imposed upon us."

"I hope you're right. It still sounds like spying." Geoffrey seemed troubled.

"I'll admit that it might prove embarrassing if we're caught. But Pinehurst is not a government installation. We will not turn over what we learn to any foreign power. Technically, the laws on espionage do not apply. And if what I suspect is true, we would be morally derelict in not finding out what is going on there."

I took the checkbook from the desk drawer and began my errands. The drive through London, even in spite of rush hour bustle, was invigorating. One by one I picked up the ingredients. They ranged from a still camera that we didn't have in stock, to aluminum tubing, to television circuitry and a rear projection screen. When I arrived back at Baker Street, I found Geoffrey hard at work putting the final touches on the plans. He looked up as I entered.

"Ah, you're back just in time. Here's a sketch of what I want. You should have more than enough material for us to get the job done. I'd like to have it finished in time to try it out at Pinehurst before the work shift ends."

"That fast? Wouldn't it be better to wait until evening?"

"No." Weston began laying out the aluminum sections on the table. "There might be less people about, but I need the lights turned on full. The room beyond will be darkened when the staff leaves."

We set to work rigging the screen on a frame, soldering connections, and putting the sub-assemblies into place. The thing came to resemble a pyramid turned sideways with a projection screen as the upended base. At the other end, where the thin metal arms came together, two cameras and the projector were mounted side by side. A pipe clamped to the spot extended downward so that the whole affair could be picked up like a campaign poster. A yardstick was glued to the pole. Wires ran down through the pipe. The entire frame was collapsible.

A pot of coffee and several hours later, the job was complete. Wires in the handle matched the color of the door. We had dug up a suitcase to hold the machine. A smaller one contained the batteries. We were ready to travel. Geoffrey called ahead to the laboratory so that they would be expecting us.

The trip to Dorking took longer than we had expected. We arrived at Pinehurst at a little after four. Who

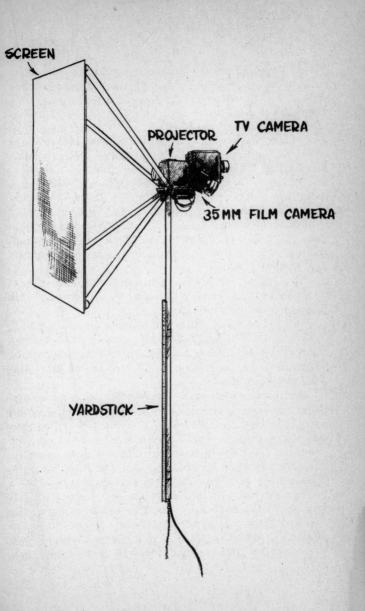

should be waiting for us at the front door of the main building but the bulbous-nosed Charles Woodward. We walked up—suitcases in hand—just in time to hear his pedagogical greeting.

"Hallo, gentlemen. Most . . . ah, industrious of you to come again. You're getting on well with everything, I trust. You got my note about the truck. Always glad to be of help. What can I do for you now?"

"Actually," Geoffrey considered, "what we'd like is to be left alone in the laboratory to finish up our examination. I don't suppose you could arrange that?"

"No trouble, no trouble at all!" Woodward chortled. "I'll just have to ring the staff first, you understand, so that they can lock the door to the restricted area."

"And the guards?"

"Yes, of course. I'll let them know that they can expect you on the screens. Will there by anything else?" He beamed upon us in anticipation.

"No," I broke in, "that will be quite all, thank you."

Weston and I, each holding a suitcase, strolled down the corridor with the acting director. At the first turn he left us to make the arrangements. By now we knew our own way by heart.

Heath's lab was just as it had been two days before. From all appearances, not so much as a beaker had been moved. Since the man's position hadn't been filled by a scientist, the room would probably remain unused for some time. We could hear sounds emanating from the laboratory beyond, but the transom was closed and the walls were solid. We couldn't make out any words.

Weston and I set our suitcases down along the left wall—near the back door and just out of range of the television camera. From this point on we spoke in whispers. It wouldn't do to have a chance phrase or two overheard by those behind the wall. From the larger suitcase Weston extracted two yardsticks.

"We are now, John, going to create an illusion. We are going to convince our watchers that we are interested in knowing every dimension of this room—to the inch."

We began measuring every conceivable distance—between wall and lamp, lamp and desk, floor and heating duct. After each measurement we carefully recorded our findings on note pads. Gradually we worked our way out of the line of vision of the camera. Once hidden, we quickly popped open the larger suitcase again and unfolded our machine—snapping each support strip into place. Next we plugged the wires dangling from the handle into the batteries in the overnight case. With the machine on, the screen itself—when seen from the front—appeared not to be there. The miniature television camera, mounted next to the thirty-five millimeter automatic, attached to a projector that flashed the image behind the machine to the screen at the front. All that was visible was a vertical yardstick below the affair—the handle.

"Now," Geoffrey instructed, "here comes the sticky part. You'll have to hold the suitcase so that it obscures the wires at least until we're in front of the door. After that they should be camouflaged by their color. If anyone in the other laboratory is looking our way, the show is over. But people do not usually look above their own eye level. The lens opening on the still camera should adjust automatically. So there's not much to worry about on that account. All I have to do is pull the chain that extends from the pipe, and we'll get some dandy pictures."

Weston walked to the wall—holding the equipment at a distance of perhaps a foot from it. From the guards' office we hoped it looked like he was simply holding a yardstick up to take a measurement. I carried the battery case and stood slightly behind and to his side—shielding the wires from view. We moved to the right and reached the door. The yardstick appeared to reach nearly to the top of it. The screen, of course, extended nearly to the ceiling. The film camera was now directly in front of the glass transom and aimed downward to record the contents of the adjoining room. Weston pulled the chain and we heard the reassuring click whir, click whir as the film advanced. In a matter of seconds we had shot the roll. My partner moved the yardstick back to the left and out of view of the guards' camera. In a moment we had our machine disassembled and restored to the case. We then continued making measurements with the two decoy yardsticks. Those in the observation center must, by now, have been convinced that we were going to construct a scale model of the entire room. Next we spent some time opening drawers and examining whatever we might be expected to examine. After a decent interval, we picked up our bags and walked out the way we had entered. I began to hum a song whose words I didn't know. And Geoffrey made a greeting here and there to those employees that we met in the hall. As we turned toward the exit, a voice from behind stopped us. It was that of Charles Woodward.

"Hold on there a moment, chaps!" He reached us in a few quick strides. "I don't mind telling you I was watching your work from the guards' office. Excellent! What thoroughness! You didn't miss a thing. It makes me feel better just to know you're on the job. Just thought I'd let you know, that's all."

"Thank you very much," I replied. "We tried to get everything we could."

"And you did. You did. It was a sight to see. Please come back again—anytime. Maybe when you're not in such a hurry we can sit down and talk about the case."

"But for now," Weston contributed, "we'd best be on our way. We expect some interesting developments within the hour."

Woodward accompanied us as far as the parking lot. We nonchalantly tossed the suitcases into the back of the wagon, said our good-bys, and wheeled the Mercedes slowly down the drive. At the gate we waved at the guard before leaving the grounds. Once outside, I let out a sigh.

"I certainly wouldn't want to go through that again."

"Oh, come now," Geoffrey chuckled. "You were as cool as a fish on ice. I didn't know you had it in you to tell that pun."

"And I almost died when you told yours. Humpf! Interesting developments, indeed!"

"That was simply irresistible. The man is certainly easy to please. The guards more than likely thought we were crazy. Either reaction, though, is as good as the other."

"I take it that from here we return to Baker Street and the darkroom."

"Your deduction is," Weston agreed, "impeccable."

And so we did. Shadows were lengthening as we drove along that street of town houses and shops and drew to a stop in front of our own modest lodging. I was beginning to feel rather like a commuter to the suburbs. My partner retired immediately to the darkroom. As the job could be done neither faster nor better with two sets of hands than with one I turned on the reading lamp, leaned back in the recliner, and became engrossed in Dickens' tale of the seven poor travelers. After a time I closed my eyes. It seemed but a moment before Geoffrey's hand on my shoulder awakened me. He was excited.

"John, here it is! Here's the final link. We've got him now."

He was waving a photograph in front of my face.

"Hold it still a minute," I begged. "Let me see it." I reached out the steadied his hand. "Good heavens! The place is lined with fish tanks filled with babies. How monstrous! They've killed the lot of them!"

"No," my friend corrected. "Look at the umbilical cords. The foetuses are, I believe, alive."

"No wonder they want to hide their foul deeds," I declared grimly. "This is inhuman. Englishmen would never stand for it."

"You forget that Englishmen are."

"Some of them."

"True. Only a few—for now."

Tiny, naked bodies curled in balls and hung suspended amidst the liquid and bubbles of artificial wombs. Scientists looked on approvingly. I wondered who the babies would call "mother." Perhaps the state!

CHAPTER 8

To Catch a Snake

Weston dressed himself that evening in an outlandish costume—complete with a black cape. By the time that he applied makeup, he was a character straight out of the Middle Ages. As Shakespeare would have said, he had a "lean and hungry look." I had a feeling that he was not going to a party. His words confirmed my suspicions.

"Taylor, what I'm about to do is more than a little dangerous. But I believe it's necessary. I would appreciate your prayers. Don't expect me back before morning."

I looked him over critically and added a touch of shadow to his eyes. "Are you armed?"

"No. I have to expect a search. This face and a friend who's coming along will have to suffice as my protection. You remember Clifford Webb—the fellow we rescued from the Druid priests? He still has some of his old connections, and he's agreed to be my guide."

"You're going to infiltrate a Satan cult then?"

"Yes, I'm afraid so," he admitted.

"Won't your presence keep the rituals from working?"

"Perhaps. I'll try to leave before the filthy part. If I can't, I'll simply have to trust the Lord to keep my presence a secret."

"And there's no other way?"

"I wish there were."

A honking outside announced the arrival of the taxi. Weston grabbed his cane and hurried out the door.

I waited up late that evening—worrying, listening to the quad, and (as Geoffrey had requested) praying. The ticking of the cuckoo clock seemed to grow louder as the night wore on.

I must have been dozing, for I started at the sound of the key turning in the lock. The darkness in the street was beginning to lighten into the grey of dawn. I could hear my friend's shoes squeak as he crossed the threshold.

"No need to be quiet there, Geoff. I'm awake."

My colleague came out of the shadows into the lamplight. I gasped. His face was discolored, and blood was trickling down from over his eye.

"I fear," he apologized, "that I have had a little accident."

He crumbled onto the sofa and fought to get his breath. I ran to the kitchen, wet a dishrag, and searched around for a tube of antibiotic cream. Returning, I bathed Geoffrey's face as best I could. Fortunately some of the bruises washed off. Others did not. The cut was a nasty one. But repairs were soon completed. The bandage was effective but not particularly artistic.

"What in the world happened to you? Are there any other injuries? Should I call a doctor?"

Weston looked up at me and smiled weakly. "Oh, no. It's nothing serious. I'm just one big study in black and blue. Would you believe, John, that the night went beautifully—without a hitch. Then on the way home I was robbed by a gang of London billies. I think I'll sleep on the couch. Please turn out the light before you leave."

Almost immediately his even breathing told me that he had fallen asleep. I brought a blanket from the cedar chest, covered him up, and then retired for the night.

It was one in the afternoon before Geoffrey stirred. I had been up for some time, trying to be as inconspicuous as possible. Soup was heating on the stove when a groan from the living room declared that one G. Weston had returned to the land of the living. It was my turn to put the coffee on the table. My friend emerged from the living room like some battle-scarred Roman gladiator limping from the field of combat. He tried to smile but winced.

"It's a pity, John, that this didn't happen on All Hallow's Eve. I might win a prize for the costume."

"Or you might be thrown into gaol as a suspicious character," I pointed out. "Have you any idea who did it?"

"I'm afraid I did it to myself. It was my own stupidity. I saved Clifford the bother of driving me home and was walking the few blocks to the tube station."

"Then it was literally a gang that attacked you?"

"Oh, most assuredly," Geoffrey admitted. "There were eight or eleven of them coming from both sides. If I hadn't been able to back against a building and get in a couple of licks with the cane, I think they would have killed me. I was lying in a flower garden when someone lit the porch light and frightened them off.

"Did they get very much?"

"Now there's a joke. I wasn't carrying my wallet for fear of being searched. I doubt that they made off with more than three pounds." He began sipping the coffee.

"Did you notify the police?" I inquired.

"I did, but I don't believe much will come of it—aside from providing some men in the Home Office with a good laugh."

"You didn't see any faces?"

"Couldn't recognize them if my life depended on it! By an odd coincidence, the street light had been smashed.

"Then there's nothing for it," I sympathized, "but to chalk the whole thing up to experience."

"Unfortunately, I have to agree. I feel ridiculous, though—like the pugilist who slipped in the bath and broke his nose. I might be able to ask around and uncover a trail, but there simply isn't time. The matter at Pinehurst is an abscess on the neck of England. It has to be lanced, or the poison will spread."

"What are you going to lance it with?"

Weston paused for a second. His next words were solemn.

"I've got the evidence now. We're going to expose the murderer."

"Are you sure you have enough for a conviction?"

"That remains to be seen. Twigg may have to tie up some loose ends. If you'll put the soup on, I'll ring him up and see if he can arrange a meeting for us for tonight."

Geoffrey left the room and made his telephone call. From his side of the conversation, I could tell that Twigg agreed to bring all those involved in the affair together. Although the Inspector despised my partner's flamboyant methods, he invariably acceded to them. The meeting would take place at seven-thirty in the late Arthur Heath's living room.

For the next few moments Geoffrey busied himself once again with the spectroscope. After the graph was developed, he covered up his bruises as best he could with powder and informed me that he would be out for the next several hours. I was to tell callers that he would be back by six. He left whistling.

Weston returned home only seven minutes late. He was carrying a bulging envelope in his right hand, and the gleam of the chase was in his eye. I was reminded by his gait of the swashbuckling stride of a pirate. This was the climax of an adventure, and he was savoring it to the last. His first words were to the point.

"Get our things together, Taylor. There's no time for delay."

That set off a helter-skelter search for the odds and ends that we had uncovered during the investigation. With them in hand, we then headed for Reigate. As we sped down the motorway, I noticed Geoffrey's worried frown and commented about it.

"I say, you don't seem particularly confident at the moment."

"If only," he lamented, "there were more physical evidence. I've got my murderer. The question is whether I can convince the others of it."

"But you said you were going to let Twigg worry about that."

"Hang it all, John, I'm not sure that I can convince Twigg. The man's so level-headed and bullish. And the solution is so bizarre. I don't know whether he'll go for it. I may almost need a confession."

We parked in front of the brownstone at dusk. As we approached it, a light went on in the living room window. We could see from the cars parked up and down the street that we were not the first to arrive.

Mrs. Heath greeted us at the door and showed us into the room where the others were gathered. Just before we reached it, Geoffrey took her aside and whispered something to her that I couldn't hear. She nodded and hurried off into another part of the house. We continued on toward the sound of muted voices. As we entered, I surveyed the room. Some bloodstains were still spattered around the dead man's chair. Inspector Twigg was standing by the fireplace to my left, speaking with a uniformed policeman. James Smyth was seated in the far left corner. He was staring nowhere in particular and was obviously bored. Peter Heath occupied a high-backed chair by the front window. He was passing time reading a paperback novel. Niles Gilbert and Mary Starling were holding hands on the sofa. Charles Woodward paced about like an expectant father. Even as I watched, Tom Yancy and Earl Garfield strode into the room—completing the guest list. Mrs. Heath now returned from her errand, handed Geoffrey what looked to be a small photograph, and then offered the two guards some folding chairs which she must have brought out of the closet for the occasion. As the last of the visitors settled down, conversation withered away to silence. Twigg now took the lead in getting things underway. He stepped to the center of the semicircle and spoke out forcefully.

"As you know, three very strange...ah...incidents have occurred in as many days. The Yard had been making diligent inquires. And, due to the insistence of the late Dr. Heath, Mr. Weston has also lent a hand. We know that the person who stole the papers from Pinehurst Laboratory got in and out by some kind of clever optical illusion. But we don't have any idea how he—or she—eluded the guards outside the building. We know that Mr. Gilbert was somehow induced, while in a yoga trance, to attempt suicide. But we don't know why, how, or by whom. We suspect on the basis of what happened to Gilbert that there was foul play in the death of Arthur Heath. We likewise note that a dog at the laboratories went mad seemingly without cause. Mr. Weston has turned over to us casts of tire markings which he discovered near the Pinehurst grounds. The tires were subsequently found in a fenced-in and locked new car lot less than a mile from here. In short, the deeper we have gone into the investigation, the more puzzling matters have become. Mr. Weston, although slightly the worse for wear today, . . . hem . . . has asked for this meeting so that we can clarify the situation a mite. Geoffrey—"

"Thank you, Inspector." Weston got to his feet and offered Twigg his chair. "Does anyone here object to these procedings being recorded?"

Smyth shrugged his shoulders. Niles Gilbert shook his head. No one said anything. I switched on my portable Crown and began taping the conversation. Weston continued speaking.

"As you know, Taylor and I have made a careful inspection of the laboratories. From that investigation we have concluded that there were three primary difficulties in carrying out the robbery. As the Inspector has pointed out, the first was the matter of entering and leaving both the buildings and the grounds without being seen. The second was the problem of opening two locked doors in order to reach the safe. The third, obviously, was the task of opening the safe.

"Let's examine the last difficulty first. The only person who had the combination to the safe was Arthur Heath. Since it is the kind of safe which has a changeable combination, not even the manufacturer would know the correct sequence of numbers. It is, quite simply, not an easy safe to crack. An expert equipped with listening devices might, in time, hit upon the combination. But we may dismiss that possibility as being unlikely. The need for a speedy conclusion of the burglary rules out a safe man entirely. It is more likely, therefore, that Heath robbed his own safe."

I noticed Susanna Heath bite her lip. Niles frowned. All eyes were on Geoffrey.

"But there is," my partner declared, "a fatal flaw in that theory. Physical evidence proves conclusively that someone entered the laboratory by employing an illusion. Since Arthur Heath could come and go at will, there was no reason for him to sneak about."

Mrs. Heath visibly relaxed.

"Since Arthur Heath did not rob his own safe," Geoffrey concluded, "someone else must have known the combination. There are, I believe, three ways that our thief could have gotten the information. The first, and most obvious, is that he or she had access to the videotape record of the laboratory. Enlargement of those portions showing Heath opening the safe might reveal the numbers that he dialed. There is—"

"Now see 'ere!" Tom Garfield interrupted. He was all but spitting venom. "Me and Tom 'as charge o' them. And there's no man what's going to call me a thief and get away with it. We keep 'em until the end of the day. Then we erase 'em. So if yor sayin' that the combination came from off o' the tapes, yer accusin' us or the day guards. I won't stand for it!"

"Then sit down," Geoffrey commanded in an icy tone. His gaze bored into the hapless guard until the man wilted and returned to the seat which he had momentarily vacated.

"As I was saying," Weston resumed, "the combination might have been gleaned from the tape. But that is unlikely for the reasons that Mister Garfield has just expressed. Both he and Tom Yancy, as well as the rest of the guard force, have undergone polygraph tests. And, while it is possible to beat the lie detector, I don't believe that that has happened in this case.

"The next possibility is that Arthur Heath had written the combination down on a sheet of paper and placed it in his wallet. If so, one would tend to suspect those closest to him—his family and close friends. They would be the most likely to have access to his wallet. Or it might have been a pickpocket."

Weston surveyed the group critically. Peter Heath had laid aside his novel. Niles and Mary seemed to have forgotten that they were still holding hands. The silence was absolute. My partner picked up the deductive thread.

"There is also the possibility that the information was extracted directly from Heath's mind. If, indeed, he died as a result of mental manipulation, might not that same manipulation have been used for obtaining the combination? But, if so, what method was used? Drugs are a possibility. Hypnosis is a possibility. Some other form of persuasion may also be envisioned. If drugs, anyone could have done it. If hypnosis, then once again we zero in on close friends as being the most likely suspects. A total stranger will have little opportunity to mesmerize the head of a research project.

"Now if hypnosis was the method employed in discovering the combination, it in all likelihood was also the instrument used for driving Heath to suicide and Gilbert to attempted suicide. If that is the case, then we are left with very few suspects indeed. Mrs. Heath could have hypnotized her husband, but she had no contact with Niles the night that he started shooting. Peter Heath, likewise, could not have hypnotized both people. It might be argued that a post-hypnotic suggestion could have been triggered for one or both of the men by a telephone call. But John and I heard no telephone ring at Mr. Gilbert's house 'from the time he entered it until the shots forced us to action. There is an off-chance that Niles' attempt could have been set to go off by the clock. But if that were the case, then he would have had to be hypnotized and given the suggestion that very day—at some time after he spoke with me. There was no opportunity for that. While Niles was at work, he was with people who are unlikely as burglars since they already had access to the information which the hypnotist would have stolen. They would, therefore, not be the hypnotist. And their presence would prevent Niles being put under by someone calling him on the telephone. From the time he left Pinehurst, he was accompanied by his fiancée. He had no contact whatsoever with either Mrs. Heath or Peter. Miss Starling, did Niles seem at all odd before he drove home?"

Mary Starling adjusted her skirt. "No, Mr. Weston, he did not. And there were no telephone calls. We were listening to records."

"Thank you. So it is certain that neither Susan nor her son hypnotized Niles. On the other hand, Mary, you did have the opportunity to do so. You have no doubt learned about trances from your boyfriend. He would have demonstrated yoga exercises to you. If, unknown to Mrs. Heath, you were having an affair with her husband, you would have also had the opportunity to hypnotize him in his sleep or by the use of drugs. Your claim to having been with Niles at the time of the theft would then be explained, not as an attempt to supply him with an alibi, but as a grasping for one for yourself!"

Mary Starling had turned deathly pale. Niles Gilbert, at her side, was plainly furious.

"There is *no* triangle!" he fairly shouted. "And she has never so much as watched my exercises!"

"There are, of course, several things," Geoffrey continued completely unruffled, "which make me doubt Miss Starling's guilt. For one thing, Arthur Heath (on the night of the murder) told me that someone had made impressions of his keys. Mary would not have needed to do so, since she already had identical keys for use at work. She might have suggested to Heath that he throw a red herring in my path, but I rather doubt it. More to the point, I have determined that stealing the Pinehurst papers would have required a person of exceptional physical strength. Miss Starling's figure, while very admirable, is simply not well enough muscled to have carried it off.

"That brings us to Niles. He is, of course, the only one here who has openly advocated the use of trances. We have only his word that Dr. Heath laughed at yoga. For all we know, he could have initiated Heath into the practice, suggested that the man kill himself, and then have attempted to throw us off the trail by pretending to commit suicide himself with a pistol which he knew to contain blanks.

"Again, however, there are problems. Mary may be too weak to have stolen the papers. Niles is certainly strong enough, but he is too large. Physique plays an important part in this case. Niles Gilbert could have easily carried around the machine which was used in entering the laboratory; but if he had been in it, the machine would have been too tall to fit through the door. What is more, it is most unlikely that he would have noticed that the bullets in the gun were blanks. He had no reason to look at the pistol unless he thought they were blanks, nor a way to tell they were blanks without looking at the gun." Weston bowed slightly in Niles' direction. "And so, Mr. Gilbert, I deduce that you are not the murderer."

"How very big of you," the scientist shot back with biting sarcasm. "I shall be eternally grateful."

Twigg had been following the line of reasoning with rapt attention. His face and arms recreated in flesh the attitude of THE THINKER. He was not happy.

"Hold on a minute there!" His voice was booming—his eyebrows slightly raised in speculation. "Weston, I've followed your logic with great admiration, but there must be something wrong somewhere. You've just run out of suspects! Everyone here either has keys, has knowledge of the experiments, could not have used the equipment for getting into the laboratory, or could not have hypnotized Niles Gilbert. And aren't you overlooking a bit? You said that nobody called Niles on the telephone and, perhaps, said some trigger word that caused the man to go into a trance. You didn't hear the telephone ring. But what if *Niles* was the one who made the call? Someone could have asked him to call, and then made him forget that he had. If that's so, then we still have some suspects in the running."

"Good to see you're thinking, Inspector," Geoffrey beamed. "I would be inclined to agree with you except for one thing. We're still left with the problem of the dog. The thief was responsible for the death of the animal. He had to be. He couldn't risk being detected by his scent. Yet the German shepherd was not drugged. And I defy you to hypnotize any animal and command it to act insane! Since hypnotism as an hypothesis will not explain all of the facts, I am inclined to reject it as an explanation of any of them. And if it is rejected, then there was no need for a telephone call.

"There must be some other kind of mental control which explains the aberrant behavior of both Heath, Gilbert and the dog. We have only to determine what it is. Let's set the matter aside for a moment and then come back to it. A look at some additional facts might give us perspective.

"The question of the keys is most interesting. Heath told me someone had made impressions of his set at a Rugby game. He may or may not have been lying. If he was telling the truth, then the finger points toward an outsider. But if the impressions were made in Heath's home—or if no impressions were really made at all—then the man was shielding someone close to him.

"Let's turn now to the last (or was it the first) difficulty I mentioned that the thief experienced in stealing the papers. He had to create the illusion of invisibility. Now some of you might wonder why such a thing would even be necessary if the person had the ability to control people's minds. There are several possible answers to that. The videotape machines could not be so controlled. The thief might not have been able to control more than one mind at a time. Some minds might not have been susceptible to domination."

Geoffrey now took an envelope from a pile that he had placed on a table beside him. He extracted an object and held it up before the group. The harsh glare of the overhead bulb gave it just enough sparkle to be seen.

"This," my partner emphasized, "is a glass bead. It was found at the scene of the theft. It is a most unusual bead with unique optical qualities. With it, and other suitable equipment, one can manufacture a machine which makes him literally invisible. I have constructed a crude model which does not incorporate the bead. It will, at least, give you an idea of the principle involved. John, will you help me set things up?"

Charles Woodward came forward to assist me, but I declined his offer. We had the device assembled in two shakes. It was, of course, none other than the projection screen which we had used in taking pictures of the inner room. I noticed that Niles—for the first time—was looking at Geoffrey and myself with a measure of respect. We had captured his interest—and no doubt the sting of my colleague's attack on Mary Starling had worn off.

"You will notice," Geoffrey continued, holding the machine high over his head, "that the equipment behind the screen is hidden from view while the rear wall is projected onto the front surface. The illusion is thus created that the machine is not there. The invention used in the robbery created the same illusion from *every* angle. The thief was capsulated, as it were. Memory curcuits froze the picture while the safe was being opened.

"As I have already pointed out, the machine was heavy. Neither of the ladies could have used it. And from the size of the marks it left on the floor, I conclude that there would not have been enough knee room for Niles to have crouched in it. The technical genius of the machine also excludes many of you from having made it. Tom, you and Earl understand the rudiments of videotape, but this thing is beyond you. And, of course, you offer an alibi for each other. You were in the guards' room when the capsule was used. Mr. Woodward, I rather suspect that you lack the necessary training also."

"Right about that, Mr. Weston," Charles readily agreed. "Right about that. There's no time to study. Business, you know."

Geoffrey cleared his throat and took a sip of water before continuing.

"During our search of this very room after Heath's death, John and I found this object implanted in the rug." Weston removed a speck from a second envelope. "You will notice that it is also a glass bead—identical in every respect with that one found at Pinehurst. In the basement of this house, if you care to look, you will find evidence that Dr. Heath was using them in optical experiments. For now let us assume that four people besides the doctor watched or took part in those experiments. Mrs. Heath and Peter—since they live here—must have known something of what was going on. Niles and Mary, I understand that you also took part in the work on occasion."

Mary Starling was nodding her head. "That's true, Mr. Weston. Niles and I did sometimes help Arthur out. But what we did was on nowhere near the level that you're talking about."

"I'm sure it wasn't," Geoffrey agreed. "Now others may have known of the experiments or have had access to the basement. But if so, we don't know who they are.

"I will now draw your attention to the tire tread which Inspector Twigg mentioned in his opening remarks. There are really two remarkable puzzles with respect to the tracks. The first is this: If the thief knew that he made the tracks, why didn't he destroy them? And conversely, if he didn't know he made them, why would he switch tires? The tires, incidentally, were originally on Mr. Gilbert's pickup. The only logical explanation is that the thief did not know he had made the tracks until sometime after the robbery. Then, fearing that the police might already have discovered them, he had no recourse but to exchange tires."

Weston paused dramatically—looking from face to face. He then took a large envelope from the evidence pile and tore open one end. His words now fell with the methodical force of a blacksmith's hammer on the anvil.

"In this photograph, ladies and gentlemen, you will find the motive for both the burglary and the murder!" He drew an eight-by-ten glossy from the envelope and held it up in front of the group. The reaction was instantaneous and violent. Charles Woodward was the first to his feet.

"Where did you get that? I'll have you in prison for

this, Weston! There are people here who have no right to see that picture!"

It was with effort that Weston held himself in check. His face muscles tightened, but he spoke softly. "But they've already seen it. So sit down and shut up." He handed the photograph to Twigg. "You may be interested in this, Inspector. I believe that there are some health regulations being broken here. It seems to me that babies are usually cared for in hospitals by medical doctors with appropriate degrees."

Twigg's brow was furrowed as he received the picture. He swallowed hard and shook his head in revulsion.

"Now where was I?" Geoffrey continued. "Oh, yes. I was talking about motive. I suspected from the beginning that 'test tube babies' might be the object of the laboratory's research. It was either that or bacteriological warfare—judging from the staff's fear of exposure even after the papers were stolen. And that same secrecy convinces me that Pinehurst was not developing artificial wombs with the purpose of saving the lives of the prematurely born. Instead, it was delving into the sinister."

"It was doing nothing of the sort!" Woodward interrupted. "We were exercising our right to . . ." His voice trailed off in the face of Weston's glare.

"Charles," Niles declared, "you're a pompous windbag. Settle down and give the man his say. I've never been overjoyed, myself, about what we were doing."

"Thank you," Weston acknowledged. "For those of you who don't know, cloning is a technique for reproducing an adult from one of his body cells. It differs from normal reproduction in that there is only one parent. The cloned child, therefore, has a genetic structure identical to that of his parent. The foetuses in the photograph were cloned.

"Twigg, you may be interested in exploring the legal ramifications of that. A clone is produced by cutting the nucleus out of a fertilized egg and replacing it with the nucleus from an adult cell. The operation is, for all intents and purposes, murder of the baby contained within the original cell—murder and depersonizing.

"That's only your personal opinion," James Smyth retorted. He smiled condescendingly. "Surely you're not bigot enough to try to force it on everyone else."

Weston sighed pityingly. "And surely," he countered, "you're not bigot enough to impose your view on the baby. But I think that even today's misguided and relativistic courts will agree with me. As perverted as the abortion laws are, they at least demand that foetuses which can survive outside of the mother be given the chance. Since you've developed artificial wombs, that single cell could survive. But you butcher it.

"And," Weston looked expansively about him, "did you scientists ever consider the theological implications of the operation that you have been performing? How does one transfer a soul? . . . Are you a materialist, Smyth?"

"I am."

"Then you haven't even worried about it. Did it slip off your knife? Can it be duplicated by adult cells? Is a whole soul in every cell, or is it in the sum total? Do little souls die every time your skin peels? Or is there something unique about a soul that allows it to be transferred in only the way that God has chosen for it to be? Smyth, what if your operation is nothing more than a desouling?"

"What," James Smyth asked woodenly, "is a soul?"

Exasperation showed on Geoffrey's face. "Look it

up!" he suggested. "Try the dictionary, a Bible, or a theology text! You remind me of a man who once asked 'What is truth?' If you really want to see what a soul is, look at the souled. The look at the soulless. Subtract the second from the first. What you have left is the essence of humanity."

Woodward broke in. "Those are pretty words, Weston. But what you suggest is impossible."

"It's not only possible, Charles, but essential. That difference is the motive for the taking of the papers and for the murder."

"I don't believe it."

"You, Mr. 'Acting Director,' had better believe it," my partner responded. "You are as responsible for the death of Heath as is the murderer. You and the board had better make some changes. Now let me put flesh on my subtraction problem."

With deliberation Geoffrey held up another photograph so that all could see. It was curled at the edges, and slightly yellowed.

"Mrs. Heath was good enough to give me this picture when we arrived this evening. It was taken of Arthur Heath when he was a teenager. You will notice, Peter, that he looks very much like you. He looks, in fact, *exactly* like you. Now doesn't that strike you as being odd—since you took pains to let us know that you are an adopted son?"

We all looked from the photograph to Peter Heath sitting by the window. He was as birdlike as his father. The similarity was, indeed, remarkable—except that now his eyes betrayed a coldness that I had never seen in the doctor's.

"There are," the youngster observed in a level voice, "such things as coincidences."

"Ah yes, coincidences." Geoffrey's disgust was evident. "But at a certain point coincidences begin to become a little more than that. Pinehurst Laboratory was first opened eighteen years ago. You are, I believe, seventeen. Figuring in tank time, I would say everything fits almost to the month.

Peter was now plainly furious. "If you want an explanation of the resemblance, Mr. Weston, I advise you to investigate my father's liaisons. I swear to you that I am not a clone. If you don't believe it, give me a lie detector test."

"You really want one?"

"Yes."

Geoffrey held him in a steady gaze. "Then repeat after me: 'I am eleven feet tall.' "

"What kind of game is this?"

"You want to prove your identity, Peter. Say it."

"All right, if you insist. But I think it's silly. I am eleven feet tall."

"Thank you," Weston responded. "You will remember that you, along with the others, gave John permission to record this meeting. There is an instrument known as the 'psychological stress evaluator' which the Yard has used for several years with modest success. It analyzes tape recordings of the human voice and detects the minute frequency changes which result from the stress of telling a lie. Do you want to bet, Peter, that the machine will say you were telling the truth when you said you were eleven feet tall? You see, if you haven't any soul, why would you show any guilt reaction? If Twigg gives you several hours of tests, he'll never find a lie, will he?"

"That won't be necessary," Niles interrupted. "The boy's a clone. There were only a few of us who knew, and most of us are gone now."

"You said you'd never tell," Peter snapped.

"I don't think that promise to Arthur is valid anymore, Pete."

Susanna Heath began to sob softly. She was among those who had not known. Peter was livid as he lashed out.

"What if I am a clone, Weston? Why ruin my future by saying so? What business is it of yours?"

"Oh," Weston beamed, "it's every bit my business. You see, Peter, you're the murderer."

"You're mad!"

"Angry, yes, but not mad. You were clever, I'll grant you that. But you made several fatal errors."

"Such as?" the youngster asked sarcastically.

"Such as changing the tires. You remember that I said the thief must not have discovered he'd left tracks until later. I found the tracks the morning after your father died. At that time the truck tires had already been switched. The robbery had taken place a little after midnight the day before. Therefore, the burglar must have discovered the tracks at some time during the morning or afternoon following the theft. I checked at the gate. You and Niles were the only two who came to the laboratory that day. Since we've already established that Niles could not have stolen the papers, it must have been you."

"That's a public road," Peter challenged. "It could have been anybody. Or whoever it was might have worried that there might be tracks without ever seeing them."

"True," Geoffrey conceded, "but isn't it more likely that the trip jogged your memory? You looked at the side of the road, and there they were."

"No."

"Who else but you would even be concerned about the tracks—let alone switch tires? If the thief were a stranger, he wouldn't concern himself with hiding the fact that a certain stolen car had been used. There would be no link to him. Of those who at one time or another either drove the truck or were given driving lessons in it, neither your mother, Niles, nor Mary are physically capable of the crime. You are the only one who is young, short, strong, and who has had access to the pickup. Since the driving lessons linked you to the truck, you had to change the tires so as to hide the fact that the truck had been used."

"But what motive could I have for stealing the papers in the first place?"

Weston smiled disarmingly. "What motive, indeed! Peter, you were the *only* one with a real motive. Some of the scientists might have wanted to stop the laboratory's work, but they could have done that by picking up the telephone and calling the press. Money was not a factor. Nor was the desire for information. But, young 'man,' there was someone with a secret he wanted to hide." My partner picked up a well-stuffed envelope from off the table. "I have here your school records and the observations of the headmaster. It seems that the general consensus is that you are amoral. And those who offend you are in the habit of having accidents. You didn't steal the papers to obtain information, but to prevent others from learning about you. Dr. Heath had kept records of your development. He may have still been running some tests. And he was suspicious of you. But the papers had to disappear before your father could be eliminated. You didn't steal the papers to prevent research, but to insure it. You were the prototype protecting your incubus brothers. You stole additional papers to hide the real reason for the theft.

"You're a liar!" Peter shouted.

"I saw you last night," Geoffrey replied. "The other

members of the coven say you have extraordinary powers. Do you see this piece of fused glass?" He held it up. "I found it in one room of the abandoned building in which you were meeting. Its spectrograph is identical to that of the beads. I'm sure that Twigg will be able to find bits and pieces in the wreckage which will further prove that it was your machine.

"Then there are the ladders that you used to scale the fence to the car lot. I imagine we might find some scratches on them which match the jagged peaks at the top of the fence. You do have a couple of ladders around here, don't you?

"And your I.Q. is absolutely phenomenal, Peter. It is, one might say, inhuman. Your method of forcing your father to kill himself was ingenious. You told him *what* you were. So much for any last shred of faith in the future that he might have had. Then you forced him to think of the hopelessness that lay at the end of his view of life. You kept it up until he could no longer stand to live. It was easy, wasn't it? After all, he was a bit of an obsessive-compulsive anyway. But it wasn't hypnosis, was it—either with your father or with Niles? You worked it with Niles without even coming near. IN THE NAME OF JESUS CHRIST, I COMMAND YOU TO ANSWER. WHO ARE YOU?

All of our eyes were fixed on Peter Heath in fascination. He sat there next to the table just as before, but slowly his lips quivered into a snarl. I had the sensation of confronting a rabid dog. His back and neck contorted until he scarcely seemed human. Peter surveyed Weston with a long, perverted leer. And then I heard the voice. It began as a cackling giggle. Saliva drooled from between bared teeth. A halting, rasping, hollow hiss breathed an ancient message: "I AM LEGION, FOR WE ARE . . . MANY."

All of us were as still as statues—stunned by the words. We stared transfixed into the pit of hell. I could feel my skin crawl. Mary Starling began to scream. Then Weston's yell jolted us to action.

"Get hold of his arm! Don't let him get that knife! Pin him down!"

Niles, Geoffrey, and I all made a dash for Peter. Perhaps it was that split second of paralysis. We arrived too late. He picked up a letter opener from the table and very deliberately pushed it into his heart. Then he smiled at us and silently toppled to the floor. There his blood mingled with that of his father. The case of the invisible thief was closed.

EPILOGUE

A little after midnight Geoffrey, Twigg, and I sat around the kitchen table at 31 Baker Street and talked about the case over a late snack. I was most concerned about the remaining clones.

"What's to become of them now, Twigg? They're nothing more than empty houses for demons."

"I don't know," he confided. "Woodward says he'll see to it that they're destroyed. But I suppose I'll have to keep him from doing that until we can get a court to rule that they're not human."

"Which," Geoffrey observed, "will be the court case of the century."

"It will, indeed," the Inspector concurred. "But with the bits and pieces of evidence you unearthed, along with the recording and the testimony of those who saw Peter Heath's last moments, I think we'll win it."

"There are a couple of things, though," I admitted, "that still baffle me. If Peter could control Arthur Heath, why didn't he use his father to steal the plans? And if Peter was possessed by demons that could communicate with others that hovered about the minds of Niles and Arthur, why didn't they know that we had removed the slugs from the bullets? Why did they force

Niles to attempt suicide?"

Weston took a sip from his coffee cup and looked thoughtfully at the window.

"Perhaps," he reflected, "the demons could not really get control of Arthur until he consciously repudiated Christianity in his talk with me. Remember that once a king said some prideful words, and his hair grew as long as eagles' feathers. Man and devil are not alone in this universe. As for the missing slugs, I guess they remind us that Satan is not as clever as he would like others to think he is. I was praying from the time we left Niles at the laboratory until we walked back out of his house. God evidently did not allow the demons to know what we were doing. That is my only explanation, also, of why Peter didn't recognize me at the assembly of the witches. He must have been in some manner blinded.

"One last thing," I asked. "Who shot at us?"

"We'll probably never know," Geoffrey admitted. "Peter might have controlled someone else and forced them to make the attempt. Or it could have been a member of the coven. Perhaps we simply have enemies."

"And what," Twigg wondered, "will become of the idea of an invisibility machine?"

"Oh," I replied, "I suppose mankind will rediscover the fine points of Peter Heath's technology soon enough. And we will engineer weapons with it. Can't you visualize invisible tanks. Ouch! And there will be spies roaming about at will. And don't forget the bombs of groups like the old "provisionals" popping out of nowhere!"

"You're probably not far wrong." Twigg shook his head in resignation. "I think I'd like to hear a little more about Jesus Christ."

"With pleasure!" I took a bite from my jelly muffin. "After all, we've got all night."

DATE DUE

1990			
1991			
1992			
(1993)			
DEC 0 8			
(1994)			
DEC. 21			
1-20-95			
(95)			
(96)			
(97)			
(98)			
(99)			
(00)			
(01)			
02			